"I could break your neck and make it look like a fall," Patrick said

His voice was like silk. He reached out and slid his hand along the side of her neck, up under her hair. "It wouldn't take that much to arrange."

Molly swallowed. His skin was warm, rough and oddly erotic against her neck. "Wouldn't the police be suspicious?"

"I could handle them."

Molly looked at Patrick then, directly into his dark, stormy blue eyes, and a little frisson of fear danced down her spine. Followed by something else.

He could kill. She believed that of him.

As his head dipped toward hers, blotting out the light, she knew she shouldn't let him kiss her. And yet she would—in spite of the danger....

FROM THE EDITORS

Enigmatic heroes, electrifying romance and breathless suspense have been quintessential trademarks of Anne Stuart novels for more than two decades. And readers can't get enough of her books. Harlequin Intrigue is proud to have published Anne's work, and notes with pride that *Winter's Edge* was a Romance Writers of America RITA Award winner. We look forward to bringing you more fabulous stories from this incomparable and accomplished author.

ANNE STUART

WINTER'S EDGE

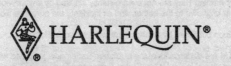

TORONTO • NEW YORK • LONDON
AMSTERDAM • PARIS • SYDNEY • HAMBURG
STOCKHOLM • ATHENS • TOKYO • MILAN • MADRID
PRAGUE • WARSAW • BUDAPEST • AUCKLAND

ISBN 0-373-83422-5

WINTER'S EDGE

Visit us at www.romance.net

Printed in U.S.A.

Prologue

She was coming back. The cunning little tart had managed to fool them all. She'd survived the blow on the head, the coma. So far she hadn't said a word, but there was no counting on that happy state of affairs to continue.

She had a reason for her silence, there was little doubt of that.

She would have to die. Sooner or later. Before she decided to start talking. Before she decided to turn the tables, and try her delicate hands at a little extortion. She would have to die.

The only problem was how to arrange it. Make it look like an accident? Or make it look like someone else had murdered her...

That would be the most delicious of all. Kill two birds with one stone. She would die. And he would be blamed.

Ah, life could be very sweet indeed.

SHE WAS COMING BACK. He had no choice in the matter, Patrick Winters thought as he slammed around the empty kitchen. She'd been hurt, she needed time to recover. She'd been implicated in a suspicious death, and she'd refused to answer questions. The police wanted her readily available, and he was the logical person to provide her a place to live.

He leaned back against the kitchen counter. It was just past dawn, and if he was a decent, caring man he'd be preparing to drive across the river to New Jersey, to the hospital, and fetch her back to Winter's Edge, the only home she'd ever known. She'd lived there for seven years, and she had no place else to go.

If she had, he'd gladly send her there. He never wanted to see her again, not if he could help it. She'd caused too much harm, destroyed too much, with her willful anger and childish spite. He wanted her away from here, out of his life.

Before he made the mistake of thinking there might be something else, some faint glimmer of hope.

He'd been a fool in the past. He wasn't about to let her make a fool of him again. She'd come back, spin her persecution fantasies, and then, once the police or someone was able to force the truth out of her, he'd send her away.

He had no responsibility for her. She had more than enough money, more than enough self-absorption to handle life. She could go, and he'd never think of her again.

Until he signed the divorce papers.

He wasn't going to waste his time, his day, going

after her. There were plenty of other ways to get her safely transported back to the sprawling estate in Bucks County. Someone else could do it.

In the meantime, he was getting the hell out of there. And he wasn't sure when he'd bother to come back.

Not until he could look at her, at her pale, innocent face with the green-blue cat's eyes, at her soft mouth, and not think about the past.

And how much he'd wanted her, once, long ago.

And damn it, how much he still wanted her.

SHE WAS GOING BACK. She knew it; the thought danced through her befogged mind as she drifted in and out of sleep. She felt both frightened and excited, reluctant and eager. Yet she wasn't sure where she was going, or why.

She didn't know what she'd find when she got there.

She only knew she was returning to where she belonged.

Whether they wanted her or not.

Chapter One

It was very still in the room, still and warm. Maybe
that should have reassured her, but it had the opposite effect. She fought her way out of the cocoon-
ing sleep, the too familiar feelings of panic beating
about her like the dark wings of a thousand bats.
She opened her eyes to face the sterile whiteness of
a hospital room, and she remembered nothing. Except that she was afraid.

Without moving a muscle she slowly began taking in her surroundings. Her head pounded like a
sledgehammer, and she reached a tentative hand out
to touch it, finding a tender scalp beneath a surprisingly heavy mane of hair. Drawing back her shaking
hand, she looked at it closely. It appeared neither
foreign nor familiar, a tanned, capable hand with
long fingers, short nails and no rings. And her panic
grew.

''You're finally awake then.'' A voice broke
through her tangled thoughts, and her eyes met the
warm, friendly ones of a young nurse. ''I thought
you'd sleep forever after that last shot we gave you.

You were pretty upset.'' She moved closer, her eyes cheerfully curious behind the wire-rimmed glasses. ''How are you feeling, hon?''

She hated being called hon. That little she could remember. ''Where am I?'' she demanded finally in a faintly husky voice that was equally startling. She didn't dare ask the more important question—*who am I?*

''Riverview Medical Center,'' the nurse answered, watching her closely. ''Is something wrong?''

''How long have I been here?''

''Two weeks,'' the nurse answered. ''Don't you remember?''

She shook her head numbly, and the wicked pounding increased. ''Not a thing.''

The nurse clucked with professional sympathy, her brown eyes troubled. ''Take a deep breath and try to relax. You've had several of these blank spells before—with any luck this one won't last too long. They often follow a bad concussion like you've had. Do you remember anything at all this time?'' she asked curiously, making a small notation on the chart in her capable looking hands.

''Nothing. How long have these blank periods usually lasted?'' She clasped her unfamiliar hands together in an effort to hide the tremor.

The nurse shrugged. ''They come and go. A few hours, at the most. Once it went on for several days. You just lie back and rest and I'll get the doctor to answer any more questions you might have. This is such a shame—they were planning to discharge you today if it was all right with Lieutenant Ryker.''

''Lieutenant Ryker?'' she echoed. ''Is he in the army?'' It was a stupid question and she knew it. She might not have any concrete memories, but she knew she was in trouble. Deep trouble.

''He's with the police. You've forgotten how you got in here, haven't you?'' She leaned over, taking her pulse.

The woman in the bed nodded miserably.

The nurse hesitated, glancing toward the door as if expecting help. ''You were in a serious car accident, Mrs. Winters.''

The name meant nothing to her. She glanced down at her hands, but there was no ring. No telltale mark of one recently discarded. ''How serious?'' She managed to keep her voice reasonably calm.

Once more the nurse hesitated. ''The passenger in your car was dead, and you had sustained a severe concussion and some unpleasant bruising. You were unconscious for several days, but since then you've been healing very rapidly. Except for your occasional bouts of amnesia.''

''And what does this Lieutenant Ryker have to do with all this? Did I commit a crime? Is there some question of negligence?''

The nurse busied herself with the pillows. ''You've refused to give us the name of the man who was with you. That, combined with the $350 thousand in cash that they found in the trunk of the car has raised a lot of questions. Questions you won't answer.'' She dropped her wrist lightly on the starched white sheet. "If you'd just cooperate and answer the police's questions, I'm sure they would let you go home and recover at your own pace. Sometimes it just takes time."

She stared at the nurse blankly. "I wish I could. I only wish I could."

She clucked sympathetically, patting her hand with a reassuring gesture. "Try not to worry. I'll go find Dr. Hobson. In the meantime you just rest and think about your husband."

"My husband?"

"You mean to say you don't remember him either?" she demanded, astonished. "I would have said he was almost impossible to forget."

"Is he...nice?"

"Nice?" She considered the notion. "Somehow I don't think so. As a matter of fact, the two of you don't seem to get along so well. But God, is he beautiful! I wouldn't kick him out of bed for eating crackers."

"I beg your pardon?"

"Just a figure of speech," the nurse said hastily. "I'll get the doctor."

She lay back against the starched white sheets, trying to put a tight control on the panic that was sweeping over her. She knew nothing, absolutely nothing about who and what she was, and the few little tidbits the talkative nurse had dropped made things even worse. A strange man dead? A fortune in cash? A handsome husband who hated her?

This must all be some hideous nightmare. In another moment she would wake in her own bed in...

The blankness that met her probing mind filled her with more horror than the thought of a dead man sitting beside her in her car, and she felt the burn of frightened tears stinging her eyes. *But I never cry,* she thought, blinking the tears back with a sort of wonder.

She pulled herself slowly out of bed, marveling at the exhaustion that suffused her unknown body, at the weakness in her legs. She moved across the cool, tiled floor to the small mirror above the washstand and examined herself carefully. It was a complete stranger staring back at her.

No, perhaps not complete. It was like looking at a picture of a distant relative. She didn't know the person in the mirror. But she looked vaguely familiar.

She surveyed the various parts of her. Long, honey-blond hair that could do with a thorough washing, slanted green-blue eyes, a nose too small and a mouth too large. High cheekbones and a determined chin completed the picture, yet she felt neither strangeness nor recognition. She looked to be in her early twenties, far younger than she felt. She turned away from that lost face and moved slowly back to the bed. She'd lost more than twenty years someplace. Twenty-some years, and a husband she hated.

"There you are, my dear. Feeling a bit dodgy this morning?" She could only assume this elderly gentleman in the rumpled white lab coat was her doctor, but she eyed him with patent distrust and disapproval. "I don't know whether you should be out of bed quite yet," he continued.

She sat back on the side of the mattress, watching him with a distrust that seemed natural to her. "I thought I was leaving today," she said shortly. "Surely I'll have to be able to walk?"

He raised an eyebrow. "The nurse says you've had another memory loss. I guess you've forgotten that you trust me just a tiny bit."

She stared at him. He looked more like an elderly David Letterman than a doctor, she thought vaguely. And then the realization struck her—how did she know what David Letterman looked like, when she didn't know her own face?

"How much is missing this time?" he asked.

"Everything," she said wearily. "I have no idea who I am."

He frowned. "Amnesia isn't usually like that. There should be some patches of memory, some faint traces. While you've had intermittent memory loss, there hasn't been anything this severe. You have no pressure building on your brain, no sign of any trauma other than the concussion, but perhaps another CAT scan might be in order."

"No!" she protested. "No more prodding. I just want a few answers."

"Are you certain you just don't want to go home to your husband?" he asked shrewdly.

"Of course I don't want to go home to a husband I can't even remember," she said, the anger building inside her oddly familiar. She must have spent a lot of time being angry. "Do you think that's enough to frighten me into remembering again? Maybe I'm just looking for an excuse not to have to identify the dead man in the car I wrecked.''

"You remember that?"

"No. The nurse told me. I remember absolutely nothing.'' Her voice quavered slightly—another sign of weakness that she fought back with fierce determination. She couldn't afford to show any sign of vulnerability. That certainty stayed with her.

Dr. Hobson looked at her curiously. "What happened to that fiendish temper of yours?'' he asked mildly. "You've already terrified two of the toughest professionals on this floor.''

"I'm frightened,'' she said in a tight little voice. "I can't be strong all the time.''

"Of course you can't,'' he said soothingly. "No one expects you to be but yourself.''

"Well, I expect too much,'' she said in a muffled voice.

He patted her hand. "You do, indeed. Do you think you're ready to go home? I'm worried about this recent blank spot. Chances are it will pass as swiftly as the others, but still, it concerns me.''

"If I put it off I may never be able to go back,'' she said in a quiet voice, steeling herself. "The sooner I face up to it the better off I'll be. The nurse says these blank spells don't last long. I'll probably remember everything by the time I reach home. Wherever that is,'' she added with an attempt at humor that sounded just a bit bitter.

"Out in the country, in a small horse-farming community. Bucks County, I gather. We're just on the other side of the river in New Jersey—it shouldn't take you more than an hour to get home. Depending on the traffic." He took a step back, surveying her. "It's probably a wise decision," he added. "Despite the memory lapse, you're perfectly well, and we try to get people out of the hospital as soon as we can. The insurance companies don't like paying bills any more than the rest of us."

She tried to smile at his attempt at humor, but it fell flat. "A wise decision," she repeated doubtfully, half to herself.

He was already moving toward the door. "I've given your husband instructions, but I'll repeat them to you. Don't drink alcohol, don't take drugs, don't do anything too strenuous for a while. Try not to start smoking again if you can help it—it'll kill you sooner or later."

"I smoke?"

"Not for the past two weeks. Fortunately you've gone cold turkey already, so you shouldn't even miss them. Just take it easy and give yourself time to mend."

"There…there wasn't any brain damage, was there?" she questioned nervously.

"None," he said, his voice firm. "We'll give it about a week. If the amnesia continues, or you have dizzy spells, anything at all after that, I want you to come straight back here. All right?"

She summoned up her coolest smile. "Of course," she lied.

He hesitated. "You might as well get dressed,

then. I'll send the nurse in to help you. Your clothes should be in the locker behind the door.''

She dressed quickly, surprised by the clothing they insisted was hers. The raw silk suit, the ridiculously high-heeled shoes, the leather purse. They were hers—and yet she had no sense of recognition. They felt both familiar and alien to her, as if they belonged to a different sort of person. To that stranger who bore a distant resemblance to the woman in the mirror.

She tied the silk scarf around her neck with the ease of long practice, just as the nurse returned. "Is it cold outside?" she asked in a deliberately nonchalant voice.

The nurse shrugged. "About usual for the end of March." She eyed her curiously. "You *did* know it was the end of March, didn't you?"

She smiled at her. "I do now." She glanced back at her reflection. She was Mrs. Winters, tall and leggy and well dressed, suspected of God knows what, on her way to meet her handsome husband whom she apparently hated, on a day in late winter. And she was leaving behind the only people she knew in the world.

"You know, things could be a lot worse," the nurse broke into her troubled thoughts.

"I beg your pardon?"

"You've got money. You've got your health, even if your memory's a bit patchy. Even though he's a bit older than you, your husband has to be one of the most gorgeous creatures I've seen in centuries. A few nights with him should put the color back in your cheeks.''

"I thought you said we hated each other," she protested faintly.

"Well, sometimes it's awfully hard to tell the difference between hate and love," the nurse said. "Maybe you can spend the next few weeks finding out which one it is."

"Maybe. I just hope it turns out to be the right one." She was unable to make her voice sound overly optimistic.

"If it's not, I'll give you my address and you can send your husband to me," the nurse said, straight-faced.

She finally found she could smile. "I'll be happy to."

"Oh, I nearly forgot. Lieutenant Ryker would like the pleasure of your company," she said, her voice heavy with sarcasm, picking up the discarded hospital robe and heading for the door. "Don't let him scare you—he's all bark and no bite. Dr. Hobson's told him to go easy on you, but I wouldn't count on it. Just don't let him browbeat you." She smiled. "Good luck to you."

And then she was alone once more, staring down at the shiny green vinyl floor and wondering what ghastly crimes she had committed.

None. She knew that with an instinct both sure and comforting. Unfortunately she had no memory, no way to refute any accusations.

Maybe she wasn't suspected of anything. Maybe she was just being paranoid. She looked down at her elegant clothes and considered her absent husband. Somehow she didn't think paranoia was a major part of her difficulties.

Lieutenant Ryker was more than happy to inform her what her difficulties were. He was a middle-aged man, with sandy hair, sandy eyes, and a tense manner that was slightly intimidating. Not the ogre that the nurse had painted, but no charmer either. She sat across from him in the private lounge and crossed her ankles with a casual disdain that seemed to come naturally.

"Mrs. Winters, we're releasing you into your husband's custody today—against my better judgment, I might add. You must remember that you have given your oath that you'll remain in his care until this matter is cleared up." His eyes were faintly contemptuous.

"What matter?"

"Dr. Hobson told me you have a temporary memory loss." He looked skeptical. "How very convenient for you. To summarize briefly, Mrs. Winters, you were found in a wrecked car near the Jersey coast with a dead man beside you in the passenger seat. We finally got an ID on him, no thanks to you. George Andrews. You had a concussion that may or may not have been caused by the accident, and the autopsy showed that rather than dying from injuries sustained in the accident, your companion had been strangled. Now obviously you haven't the strength to strangle a man of Andrews's height and weight. Obviously, also, you must have a good idea who did it."

"Why do you say that?" she countered swiftly. "How do you know that man didn't knock me unconscious before someone showed up and strangled him?"

"Highly unlikely, Mrs. Winters. There were signs of a struggle—you had bloodied and broken fingernails, and there was no blood on Andrews's body."

"Blood? What about DNA testing…?" From somewhere in the recesses of her knowledge came the question.

"It was your blood, Mrs. Winters," he said wearily. "And the dead man isn't your only problem. There's also the question of $350 thousand found in the trunk of your car. Your fingerprints are all over that money, Mrs. Winters. Yours and Andrews's." His voice was hard, implacable and furious. "You have refused to cooperate with the police from the first moment you regained consciousness, telling us absolutely nothing, and you still refuse to do so. We know several of your companion's aliases from a fingerprint check, but after that the trail gets cold. We know he was a criminal, Mrs. Winters. A petty, blackmailing criminal." He shook his head angrily. "Maybe your husband will be able to convince you to do the honorable thing."

And maybe you can go to hell, she thought silently, maintaining an impassive countenance. "What was I doing with this man? Where was my husband?"

"I think you can answer that far better than we can, if you wanted to. All we know of your movements is that you left your husband five weeks ago, two weeks before you turned up in that wrecked car. Perhaps you've changed your mind and feel like enlightening us?'' He didn't look hopeful.

She shook her head. ''I'm afraid I can't.'' Despite the man's hostility she wanted the same answers that he did, and she made an effort to smile politely. ''I simply don't remember. Not right now, at least. I should before long, or at least that's what the doctor assures me.''

He snorted, his contempt obvious. He must have thought she was a spoiled, frivolous creature, and yet she didn't feel very frivolous, except for this silk suit she was wearing. Had she got it from her handsome husband, she wondered, the one she'd run away from? Or from her dead lover?

''Is my husband here yet?'' she asked, dreading the moment when she had to meet the stranger who would have so much control over her life, the stranger she had run from. There seemed no way to avoid it much longer.

Apparently there was. ''He's not coming,'' Lieutenant Ryker said shortly. ''He's gotten a friend of his to come and get you. I don't imagine his feelings toward you are any too charitable right now.''

''I imagine not,'' she agreed faintly, wondering desperately what, besides a husband she hated, would await her when she arrived at her forgotten home.

The answers were there. The answers she needed, the reason she'd run.

But more than answers might await her. She couldn't picture a place, or a person. But she recognized the familiar feelings that swept over her as she contemplated her return.

Longing.

And fear.

Jane Starr

quickened familiar feelings that swept over her as
she contemplated her return.
Longing.
And fear.

Chapter Two

The car sped across the endless stretch of crowded
highway, the landscape brown, dead and dreary.
What an awful time of year, she thought gloomily.
Everything dead from winter, the spring teasingly
out of sight. She wondered dismally where she was
going. Bucks County, they'd told her. Somehow that
didn't sound promising.

"Excuse me, Officer Stroup." She leaned forward
and spoke to the thickset shoulders in front of her.
"Where is it exactly that we're headed?"

He permitted himself a stare of incredulity before
returning his stolid gaze to the fog-shrouded highway. "Come off it, Mrs. Winters. You know as well
as I do where we're going. To Winter's Edge, your
husband's farm in Belltown, Pennsylvania. In Bucks
County, where you've lived for the past seven
years."

She leaned back with a languor that came easily
to her, a languor she didn't like. She sat back up
stiffly. "Do I know you?" she asked suddenly. She
hadn't registered any sense of familiarity when

she'd been introduced to the sullen hulk of her husband's errand boy, one of the local policemen, apparently.

"Your husband and I have been friends for years," he said, but there was an undercurrent in his voice she couldn't quite define. "We could have been friends too, if you know what I mean. If you weren't so picky."

She could guess what he meant, and she shuddered. "Why didn't he come and get me?" She finally voiced the question that had been eating away inside her. There was no reason it should bother her—she didn't remember the man, so why should he have the ability to hurt her? But he did. Perhaps it was no wonder that she hated him.

"I don't imagine he wants to have any more to do with you than he can help," Stroup shot back, his thick red neck mottled with irritation. "I owed him a favor or two, so I offered to take this little chore off his hands for him. Besides, I thought you might be feeling a little less uppity after getting involved in a murder."

Her eyes met his in the rearview mirror, and there was no mistaking the meaning in them. Another shudder washed over her.

"I'm feeling as uppity as ever," she said sharply, leaning back against the seat. Her head was throbbing again, and she longed for a room hidden away from everyone. Which was just what she'd get if they proved she had anything to do with the mysterious George Andrews's murder. "And you're hardly acting like my husband's friend," she added belatedly.

He laughed, a fat, wheezy chuckle. "You should realize by now that your husband doesn't give a damn what you do and who you do it with. You made sure of that a long time ago."

She turned away, trying to shut out the sight of him in the front seat, trying to shut out the sound of his voice. Anything to still the pain in her head. Obviously Stroup believed her capable of adultery as well as murder. She wondered what she could have possibly done to alienate everyone so completely. Particularly her handsome husband.

She tried to picture him. Older, the nurse had said. Very handsome. She summoned up the image of someone gentle, smiling down at her, with faded eyes and a fatherly manner. Gray hair, slightly stooped. But the comforting image shifted, almost immediately, and the man in front of her had midnight black hair, winter blue eyes, and a cool, mocking smile that held no warmth whatsoever.

Suddenly her hands were cold and sweating, her heart was pounding beneath the silk suit, and the hairpins were digging into her scalp. Her eyes shot open, and she stared determinedly at the brown, blurred landscape. She wasn't going to let them destroy her. She hadn't before, and she wouldn't this time.

The stray memory flitted through her brain like a wisp of fog, gone before she could snatch it back. Who had tried to destroy her? And why? The past remained stubbornly, painfully blank, with only the tantalizing memory to further claw at her nerves.

The sun was setting as they pulled into a small, old-worldly town somewhere over the Pennsylvania border. The gloom of the day had worked itself up to the tangible expression of pouring rain, and she watched the dead countryside fly by the windows with unabated gloom. Heaven only knew what sort of man she was about to meet. Her husband, they told her, but how did she know whether she could believe them or not? Maybe this was all some conspiracy—maybe they were trying to make her doubt who and what she was.

If only she could believe that. She felt bone tired, her head pounding. More than anything she wanted to sink into a soft, warm bed and sleep for hours and days until this nightmare had passed. But would she be sleeping alone, or with a hostile stranger who didn't even care enough to pick her up at the hospital?

She felt the sudden sting of tears in her eyes, and she opened her expensive leather handbag, searching for a tissue. The lining of the purse still smelled of the cigarettes she'd tossed, and there was no doubt she'd once been a smoker. The smell of it made her ill.

Tucked inside were two handkerchiefs, linen and expensive. The first was very plain and masculine, and the initials, embroidered so carefully on the scrap of material, were *P.A.W.* There were pale orange streaks across the white linen, too pale to be the blood she had first suspected.

Panic filled her, swift and unreasoning, and she shoved the scraps of cloth back into the purse, no longer eager to open the Pandora's box in her lap. *M.A.W.* the other handkerchief had read. If Winters was her last name, then her first must be Mary or Magdalene or something of that sort. Though why the image of Mary Magdalene, the great whore, would have come to mind when she was looking for an identity was something she didn't want to think about. She only knew she wasn't going to let strangers convince her she was something that she wasn't.

The weather didn't choose to improve. She shivered slightly as the car pulled away through the deep troughs of water, out across the rain-swept highway, then leaned back, eyes shut, heart pounding. She didn't want to watch where he was taking her. She simply wanted to arrive, and face up to it when she had to.

It was far too easy to drift into a strangely altered state. She had no idea whether it was the result of her head injury, or whatever drugs they'd given her, or just stress and exhaustion. But as she closed her eyes she could see him, through a mist of anger and desire. His eyes, winter blue, staring at her with frustration and contempt. His mouth, wide, sexual, set in a thin line of anger.

She wanted to lift her hand, to touch him. To brush a strand of inky black hair away from his face, to soothe away the fierceness as he looked at her. If she could just explain…

But it was too late for that, she knew it. Too late for second chances, too late for the truth. She let herself sink back, into the darkness, into the forgetfulness that was a mixed blessing.

The sudden bumpiness of the road jarred her into reluctant alertness, and she sat up straight, guessing by the unevenness that they must be crossing a wooden bridge. She looked out the streaming windows at the long low building as they drove by. An old stone farmhouse loomed beside it, wet and forbidding in the glare of the headlights through the pelting rain. Stroup brought the sedan to an abrupt halt, the jolt flinging her body against the back of the seat.

"Shoulda worn your seat belt, Mrs. Winters," he said with a malicious chuckle. "Or did you *forget* that it was the law nowadays?"

Her nerves had reached fever pitch. "So arrest me," she snapped back.

"Don't I wish I could," he replied, and she had no doubt he meant it. "Maybe I'll get my chance later on. In the meantime, we're here. Home sweet home, Mrs. Winters." He leaned over the back seat. "It looks pretty deserted. You want I should see you inside?" The leer was back in his thick face.

She controlled the shiver of disgust. "I don't think so, thank you. Do I have any luggage?"

"You know that as well as I do," he answered shortly, leaning back against the seat. He smelled like stale cigarettes and yesterday's beer. "You were found in the clothes you're wearing and no sign of where you'd come from. I'm sure your husband will have plenty of other stuff waiting for you. Both of you can afford it."

She stared back at his pugnacious face, struggling to think of something suitably devastating, something that would make him flinch as he'd made her flinch. Her tired mind remained a blank. She could be cruel and cutting, she knew it with a perverse pride. At least she wasn't totally defenseless. But right now she was too exhausted and tense to find the words.

"Thank you," she murmured inanely, reaching out and opening the door into the torrent of rain.

"I'll be seeing you around," he said, before driving off and splashing her liberally with mud and water. His last words echoed unpleasantly as she stood there, and for a moment she considered running.

But where would she run to? They hadn't passed another house or a car for miles; she was out in the middle of nowhere, and the rain was like tiny pellets of ice pelting against her skin. She'd been running away when they found her. Maybe it was time to stop running. Time to face the truth, no matter how unpleasant it might be.

She moved toward the back door of the house with an instinct she didn't stop to consider, her head held low against the driving rain. Pulling at the knocker, she huddled under the tiny porch roof. There was no answer.

She knocked again, this time more loudly. The strain of the day, the wetness of her clothes and the pain in her head were all joining to make her furiously angry with a fate and a husband who had put her in such a miserable situation. She stared out at the rain-soaked landscape, sorely tempted to take off into the late afternoon downpour, never to be heard from again. But cowardice and discomfort were too much for her, she thought bitterly, and feeling like a fool she turned back and knocked one last time. "The hell with it," she muttered, as she pushed open the door and stumbled in.

It took her a moment to get her bearings. The interior was warm and dark, with the scent of lemon oil and wood smoke in the air, and there wasn't a sound other than the steady tick of a grandfather clock gracing the stone-floored hallway. Her high-heeled shoes were wet and slippery, and she kicked them off with a sigh of relief before moving down the strange hallway in her damp stocking feet. Her total lack of recognition should have disturbed her. They had told her this was her home—she had no choice but to take their word for it. For the time being all she wanted was to find someplace warm and sit down.

She found her haven at the end of the hall—a warm, cozy living room with a fire crackling in the fieldstone fireplace, sending out delicious waves of heat. There was no one in sight, and for the first time she thought to announce her presence.

"Hello!" she called out, softly at first. Then, gaining courage, she shouted louder. "Is anyone home?" There was no answer, just the hiss and pop of the fire. Sighing, she sank down in one of the overstuffed armchairs by the fire and took stock of her surroundings.

She'd never been here before, she told herself incredulously. If she had, how could she have forgotten it, how could she ever have left it? Even with the gloom of the lashing rain outside, it was surely the most beautiful room she'd ever seen in her life. The walls were of an old and mellow oak panelling, the ceiling low and comforting, with shelves of books all around. The furniture around her was old, a wonderful mix of antiques and overstuffed comfort. To her right was a gateleg table with a Chinese porcelain bowl of fresh flowers on it; across the room was a Chippendale highboy that made her ache with covetousness. And yet there was no need for envy, she realized suddenly. This was her home.

She lost track of the time, staring absently into the fire. It could have been five minutes, or an hour, before she became aware of her damp, uncomfortable condition. Her silk suit was ruined, and her entire body felt clammy and stiff despite the warmth of the fire. She decided then she couldn't wait any longer for her phantom husband—she simply had to get into more comfortable clothing.

Making her way into the back hall, she turned on the lights against the late afternoon gloom. It was an eerie feeling, wandering around this vast, strange yet familiar house. At any moment she expected some stranger to pop out of a hidden doorway, to denounce her as an imposter.

But no one appeared. She climbed slowly up the curved wooden staircase with its lovely oak planks polished to a mirror shine. At the top she stopped in confusion. There were six or seven doors leading from the long, narrow hallway, and the passage itself took a sharp turn and went down two steps into another section. She had no idea which was her room.

She explored slowly, noisily, so as to alert any possible inhabitants. But all the room were deserted. Four of the bedrooms were apparently occupied, three were just as obviously guest rooms.

It was hard to decide which room could have been hers. The first contained clothes rather like the ones she was wearing: elegant, expensive, sophisticated and very uncomfortable looking. Yet they simply weren't the sort of thing that the young woman in the mirror would really want to wear, especially at her age.

But the other bedroom's closet revealed even less likely apparel. In it were dresses belonging to an obviously elegant, well-dressed matron of indeterminate age, wearing a stylishly stout size 24.

She wandered back into the other bedroom, with no choice but to accept the fact that everything was fitting in with the unattractive picture she was building of Mrs. Winters. While the other bedrooms had beautiful old flooring covered sparingly with antique hooked rugs, hers was awash with puffy white wall-to-wall carpeting. The other rooms boasted lovely old furniture, with gleaming woods lovingly tended. Her room had a matched set of expensive ugly modern furniture, all chrome and glass at screaming odds with the lines of the old room. The drapes and bedspread were satin, and the entire effect was one of tasteless opulence. She sat down at the mirrored dressing table and stared at herself over the rows of silver-topped bottles of perfumes and creams. That slightly tanned creature with the splash of freckles across her nose didn't belong in this room, did she? Somehow she had the uneasy feeling that she did.

She got up quickly, with an air of decision. Before she could begin to fathom what was going on, she needed a shower and clean, dry clothes. Searching through the many drawers of the ugly-elegant dresser, she finally discovered one pair of ancient and faded jeans among all the silk. There was a warm turtleneck, and heavy cotton sweater, stuck at the back of the drawer, and she carted them into the bathroom, stripping off her clothes as she went. The discarded suit went into the trash can. Never again would she wear one—those suits symbolized what surely must have been the most awful day of her life. If there were any worse in the lost past, she didn't want to remember them.

It wasn't until she was scrubbing her hair that realization struck her. She had gone straight to the bathroom without a moment's hesitation. She had known where it was.

Trembling slightly, she rinsed her hair and stepped out of the shower, no longer able to deny that she had been there before. No longer could she clutch at straws, hoping they'd mistaken her for someone else. She'd just wrecked that theory by coming straight to the pink-and-white bathroom that matched the fussy tastes of the sybaritic bedroom.

She dressed quickly in the chill air, towelling her long hair dry. She grabbed a pair of heavy wool socks before she ran back down to the living room and that cozy fire, the only warm room in this vast house, it seemed. It must be the stone walls, she thought. Or perhaps her husband was a miser, or an energy freak. The temperature seemed a little extreme, even for that, but then, the lady of the pink-and-white bedroom was nothing if not pampered. Maybe the creature she used to be couldn't survive those temperatures, but the new woman she was determined to become could grin and bear it.

Her hair was almost completely dry when she heard the back door slam. It took all her self-control not to jump up in panic, and she forced herself to stay still. Her elderly husband couldn't be bothered to drive to the hospital to pick her up. Well, he could at least make his way into the living room. She was damned if she was going to go to him.

She leaned back, trying to still the sudden panicked racing of her heart. Her life was about to change. She knew it, with a bleak, desperate certainty. She heard a noise by the entrance, and she looked up, a deceptively cool expression on her face.

Chapter Three

It wasn't who, or what, she'd been steeling herself for. A giant black animal ambled into the room. He stared at her from large, mournful eyes, and from the recesses of her memory she came up with a name. He was a Newfoundland dog, large and friendly. Though the look he gave her was just a bit wary.

"Hello, boy," she said softly, holding out a hand for him to snuffle. He lumbered over, his dark eyes suspicious, and with great caution he allowed her to pat his massive, leonine head, going so far as to honor her with a lick from his large and lolling tongue.

"So you're back." A high-pitched voice, soft and unfriendly, came from the door of the room, and she jumped guiltily. He was an indistinct, shadowy figure in the half light of the doorway, and she felt no pang of recognition. An older man. He could only be her husband.

She couldn't imagine what to say to him, so she was silent. He moved into the room, his paunchy figure staggering slightly, his receding chin thrust out aggressively. He was middle-aged and flabby, with a few strands of orangeish hair combed carefully over his shiny pink scalp, and his mouth had a petulant, spoiled look about it. The nurse must have had a decidedly odd sense of humor to consider this man handsome.

His eyes were small and shrewd and light-colored in his puffy red face, looking as if they could see through all her pretenses. She had no pretenses, she wanted to cry. But she never cried, she thought, staring at him silently.

"What's this new act, Molly?" he said, lounging with what he obviously considered a lazy grace in one of the comfortable, overstuffed armchairs. She hoped, perversely, that it was still damp from her sojourn in it. "This country girl look isn't quite your style, is it? You've always been more Neiman Marcus than Eddie Bauer. Maybe you're hoping to appease Patrick with your newfound docility. It won't wash, my dear, I promise you that." There was an ill-concealed malice in his slurred voice, combined with an odd wariness on his part, a watchfulness just under the slightly drunken surface.

She edged closer to the fire, away from him. "Patrick?" she questioned innocently. Her name was Molly, then. Not bad. At least it was better than Mary Magdalene.

"Oh, come off it. You needn't play games with your old pal Willy. Haven't I always been on your side?"

From the look of him she doubted it. "Who's Patrick?" Molly questioned again, stubbornly.

Willy smirked. "Why don't you go into the kitchen and find out?" he suggested amiably. "I'm sure he's dying to see you after five long weeks."

Molly rose, reluctantly, and headed out to the hall, keeping well out of old friend Willy's reach. He looked like the type who pinches. The dog lumbered after her, obviously preferring her company to Willy's. Dogs are more discerning than humans, she thought.

She found the kitchen after only one false foray into a clothes closet. The room was huge and dark, and reaching out, she switched on the light. And then realized that although she hadn't known where the room was, she'd found the light switch without the slightest hesitation.

He'd just come in the door. He stood there, staring at her, cold, implacable anger emanating from him. The dog sensed something in the air, and he whined and moved closer to Molly, nearly knocking her over in the process. She looked up at the man across the room, and felt those familiar-unfamiliar emotions rushing through her. Longing. And fear.

He was the man from her dreams, her brief flashes of memory. Now she could see him clearly, without the fog of time, and she wasn't sure she liked what she saw.

He was handsome enough, despite his unfriendly expression. He was dressed in faded jeans and an old, torn sweater. His cold blue eyes were bitter, his mouth tight-lipped and angry. He wore his black hair long, tied at the back to get it out of his way, and drops of rain glittered in the dark mane. He looked to be in his midthirties, about ten years older than she purportedly was, and he stared at her out of those wintry eyes, an angry, beautiful man. Despite his animosity she felt a stirring inside her, a stirring she knew she hadn't felt for many men. She knew who he had to be. But she wasn't ready to accept the disturbing truth.

"So you're back," he said, echoing the words of Willy. "I never thought my wife would care to grace this—now what did you call it?—this miserable old pile of stone again."

"Your wife?" Molly echoed faintly. The word was spoken—there was no way she could avoid it any longer.

"My wife," he said, his voice like ice, cold and hard. He moved closer to her with a totally unconscious grace that was somehow sinuous and unnerving at the same time. "I gather you didn't save me the trouble and get a quickie divorce during your... vacation."

He was quite close to her by now, towering over her, and she clamped down the sudden spurt of nervousness. She was afraid of this man, and she couldn't remember why. "I...I don't know," she said, determined not to back away.

His black eyebrows shot up in disbelief, giving his cool, handsome face a harsh look. "No," he said shortly. "You would have sent the decree off to me as fast as you could. I guess you'll have to cool your heels around here until we can do something about ending this ridiculous farce of a marriage." His eyes flicked over her body contemptuously. "Why have you got those clothes on?"

"I...I was cold." She controlled the chattering of her teeth with an extreme effort, knowing that her shivering was caused by nerves as much as the chill in the air. The man in front of her, her dearly beloved husband, terrified her. And that knowledge made her angry.

"You always are," he mocked, and there was no missing the double meaning. "Why didn't you turn up the thermostat?"

"I didn't know where it was."

Those cold blue eyes looked askance at that. "You've lived in this house for seven years, dear Molly. You should have learned where it is by now."

"Seven years?" she echoed, shocked. "Have we been married that long?" It was out before she could stop it. She hadn't looked old enough to have been married for so long, but then, with all those creams and potions on her dresser upstairs, maybe she was simply extraordinarily well preserved.

His eyes narrowed in surprise for a moment. "That's right, I forgot you were playing the amnesiac. No, we have not been married for seven years. I would have killed you long ago if we had. We've been married ten months, almost to the day."

"Then why did I live here?"

"You know as well as I do," he snapped, moving away from her as if he couldn't bear to be that close. "My father adopted you when you were sixteen. He always had a habit of picking up stray relatives like you and Willy. He found his only child a major annoyance. I'd never do what he wanted, so he had to settle for other people he could control."

"We're related?" She wasn't sure that made the whole situation any more palatable.

"We're fifth cousins, something like that." He dismissed it. "Look, I'm not really interested in playing games with you tonight, Molly. It's Mrs. Morse's day off and I've got to get dinner. Why don't you go back into the living room until it's ready? Keep Willy company—you'd like that, I'm sure."

That was just about the last thing she wanted to do. She took a deep breath, deciding an attempt at cordiality might not be a bad idea. "Wouldn't you like some help with dinner?" she offered tentatively.

He stared at her with amazement. "You hate to cook," he responded flatly. "Now get out of here and leave me alone."

There was no way she could refute his statement. For all she knew she could be the worst cook in the world, so she simply left him without another word. There had to be a reason behind his rampant hostility, just as there had to be a reason why he frightened her. He didn't look as if he were in the mood to answer her questions, and she wasn't in the mood to ask.

The Newfoundland followed her back into the cozy living room, deserting his taciturn master. To her relief, Willy had departed, and she seated herself on the floor by the fireplace with the huge dog be-

side her, her brain whirling. Nowhere had she found
any sense of recognition, any feeling of familiarity.
Not to mention any sense of welcome. She almost
wished she hadn't had those two moments of knowledge, when she'd found the bathroom and the light
switch without conscious effort. It seemed to be no
more than a vain hope that everyone was mistaken,
that she didn't belong with that angry man in the
kitchen, with the leering Willy.

She leaned back against the seat of the chair and
sighed. At least she was happy in this room. She
was Molly Winters, age about twenty-three. She
sighed, and the dog moved closer, nuzzling his
lion's head under her unresisting hand. Ringless, she
noticed absently, shutting her eyes.

If only she could just relax, let things come out
on their own accord. But she couldn't. There was
danger all around. Paranoia, she thought again, trying to dismiss the fear that clawed away at her. But
it clung with iron talons.

She didn't know much about her life, but she
knew one thing. She really was in danger.

And she needed answers. Fast.

She must have dozed off. The next thing she
knew she was being called for dinner, and she
awoke with a start, disoriented, suddenly panicked.
When full consciousness came it wasn't much of an
improvement, and she rose from her uncomfortable
position on the floor, hurrying out to the kitchen.
Her stranger-husband glowered at her from his place
at the kitchen table. He gestured to a seat opposite
him and the plate of unappetizing, overcooked beef.

"Willy's gone into town for dinner," he offered shortly, sawing away at his overdone steak with a vengeance. She toyed with some lumpy mashed potatoes, obviously instant from the paper taste of them, and she nearly muttered that she didn't blame him. The vegetables were bland and tasteless, the company was hostile, and she had to force herself to eat. If this was Patrick's idea of cooking she would clearly have to remedy the lack in her education. Maybe she wasn't quite as disinterested a cook as he thought.

The silence stretched and grew, while he ate and she watched. When he was finished he got up, poured himself a cup of coffee from the pot on the back of the stove before he stalked out of the room. She stared after his tall, lean form for a long, thoughtful moment. Either her husband was an incredible pig, or she'd done something totally unforgivable. She didn't remember whether he was the forgiving type, but she wasn't sure she was ready to find out.

She cleared the table, loaded the dishwasher and poured herself a cup of coffee that resembled black sludge. For a moment she hesitated, trying to decide whether to drink it in the safe, solitary confines of the kitchen or brave the lion in his den. She was learning a lot about herself fast, and one thing she'd discovered for certain—she wasn't a coward. She followed Patrick into the living room.

He was staring moodily into the fire, one tanned, long-fingered hand stroking the dog's head, the other wrapped around his empty coffee cup. He barely glanced up when she entered, and paid no attention when she sat down in the chair opposite him.

She took a sip and shuddered, then felt his eyes on her.

"You take milk and sugar in your coffee," he said in a bored voice.

"I don't know if it would help. This coffee is a lost cause."

"Maybe you could learn to make something other than instant," he snapped back at her.

She bit back her annoyed response. "Maybe I could," she said in a neutral voice. "What's the dog's name?"

"Beastie," her husband answered, staring into the fire. Upon hearing his name the dog raised his head and looked at Molly from his soulful eyes for a moment before dropping back down with a deep, doggy sigh.

She sat back in silence, sipping on the rancid brew, before making another attempt at polite conversation. "Patrick."

He looked up, startled. "Why did you call me that?" he demanded. "You usually call me Pat. When you aren't using nastier terms."

"Do I?" she murmured absently, determined not to let him goad her. "Well, if you prefer it, I'll call you Pat."

"No, I don't prefer it." He gave her his full attention. "Listen, I think we'd better come to an understanding if we're forced to share each other's company for the next few months."

"Few months?" she echoed in a hollow voice.

He nodded grimly. "It will take that long for our divorce to go through, and I promised the police I'd be responsible for you till then. I'm a man who pays attention to my responsibilities, even the unpleasant ones, but I won't have you dragging my name into the gutter any more. You will stay on this farm with no long-term visits to any so-called friends from school. If you behave reasonably well I'll give you use of one of the cars to go shopping on occasion. I know how you love to spend money," he added bitterly, the fire lighting up his cold, handsome face. "Willy will be around to entertain you, as will Aunt Ermy. You're simply going to have to curb your jet set tendencies for a while, until I'm free of you. There are the horses, as you well know, and you might even have Mrs. Morse teach you a bit about cooking if you've decided to put on a housewifely act. But don't think for a moment that you'll fool me again. Most of all, you're to keep out of my way and out of my business. Is that understood?"

She had a temper. Dr. Hobson had warned her of it, but she hadn't seen much of it in the short time her memory had been active. During the last twelve or so hours she'd been alternately frightened and uneasy.

But right now her anger overrode any lingering nervousness that might be plaguing her. She looked at the cold, handsome man who insisted he was her husband, the man who'd just dismissed her so cavalierly, and her last attempt at polite behavior vanished.

"You'd love that, wouldn't you?" she said. "You want me to go away, keep my mouth shut, leave you alone and stop asking questions. Sorry, I won't do that. You can't dismiss me like a good little girl and expect me to be seen and not heard."

"You've never been a good little girl in your entire life," he snapped. "I didn't expect you to start now. Your so-called amnesia is only supposed to cause memory loss, not total personality change."

"My supposed amnesia?" she echoed.

"You don't think I buy that for a moment, do you? It's a little too convenient, Molly dearest. You don't usually underestimate me—I suggest you don't start now. I don't believe in your amnesia, I don't believe in your lost little girl act, and I don't believe in your country girl look either. If you want to reinvent yourself, wait till you have a more appreciative audience. You lost me years ago."

"I thought we'd only been married ten months?"

It silenced him, effectively, if only for a moment. "Get out of here, Molly."

"I'm not that easy to get rid of."

"No, you aren't," he said in a faintly menacing voice. "That doesn't mean I won't try."

"Is that a threat?"

"Take it whatever way you want."

"What I want are some answers. You can give me that much, can't you? Just a few answers to a few simple questions? That shouldn't be too much of a strain on your good nature."

He stared at her for a long moment. There was no warmth, no caring in his cold face, but a certain angry resignation. "I'll answer your questions," he said, "if you promise to leave me the hell alone once I do."

Molly sat back, an equally chilly smile on her own face. This, at least, was familiar. She'd fought with this man before. The familiarity, unfortunately, was far from comforting.

"Okay," she said. "Question number one. Why do you hate me?"

"I don't hate you, Molly," he said in a cold, weary voice. "I don't give a damn about you one way or another."

"Why not? I'm your wife."

"What makes you think marriage makes people get along? We used to be better friends before we made the stupid mistake of getting married."

"Why did we get married?"

"Youthful passion," he snapped.

"I thought you were going to answer my questions."

"Those I feel like answering. I'm not in the mood to do a postmortem on our tangled relationship."

She stared at him, frustrated. Memory might fail her, but instinct told her she wouldn't get any farther with that line of questioning.

"What is it you think I've done? What is it the police think I've done? Lieutenant Ryker said he didn't think I could have killed that man. Do they think I was an accessory? If so, does someone want to kill me? Do they think I stole that money...?"

"You had no need to steal any money," Patrick said. "You have plenty of your own."

That startled her more than anything. "You mean I'm rich?" she gasped, wondering why that notion felt so alien to her.

"Very. Why do you think I married you?"

It was a stunning blow, the effect of which she tried to hide. "How noble of you," she said lightly. "What was I doing with this strange man in the first place? Why had I run away from you?"

"I guess love's young dream had faded," he said with something close to a snarl. "You always liked older men—I presume you just decided a ten-year age difference wasn't enough. You wanted someone more mature."

"That shouldn't have been hard to find," she snapped.

She had managed to startle him. There was a light in his eyes that was almost appreciative. "Be that as it may, our marriage was effectively over. You decided to take off, and it didn't really concern me why or where you were going. I was too busy dealing with the mess you left behind."

"What mess was that?"

"I'm getting a little weary of this, Molly. Besides, you may be independently wealthy, but I have work to do."

"You don't have money?"

"This is an expensive place to maintain. I'm always in debt."

"And who inherits my money if I die?" The initials on the handkerchief were his. Why was it one of the few things in her possession? It hardly seemed as if it were a love token, given their acrimonious relationship.

His smile was cool and deceptively sweet. "Why, I do, Molly. Why do you ask?"

He knew perfectly well why she was asking, and the notion amused him. Had he tried to kill her? Had he driven her away from this place that, despite the strangeness and the hostility, still felt like home, and then followed her, murdering her lover and trying to kill her as well? He had the clear motive.

"Where were you the night of my accident?"

He laughed then, and the sound wasn't reassuring. "I have an alibi, Molly. Ironclad. I didn't try to kill you, and the police believe me. You should as well."

"Why should I?"

"Because if I tried to kill you, I wouldn't make a mistake. You'd be dead. And I'd be a very wealthy man."

"Then why don't you? It seems the logical thing to do, and you appear to be a very logical man."

"Don't tempt me," he said, but his voice was like silk, and he reached out and slid his hand along the side of her neck, up under her hair. "I could break your neck, and make it look like a fall. The stairs are winding, the floor is slate, and you're recovering from a concussion. Not to mention that convenient amnesia. It wouldn't take much to arrange."

She swallowed. His skin was warm, rough and oddly erotic against her neck. "Wouldn't the police get suspicious?"

"I imagine I could handle them," he said in a

dreamy voice. "No one likes you very much, you know."

"Why not?" She swallowed, and his thumb stroked the front of her throat, gently, with only the faintest hint of pressure.

"They don't like the way you treat me."

"And what about the way you treat me?" she countered, fighting the need to bat his hand away. Fighting the need to sway closer to him.

"They don't care, Molly."

She was too close to him. She looked at him then, directly into his dark, stormy blue eyes, and a little frisson of fear danced down her spine. Followed by something else.

He could kill. She believed that of him. He could have killed the man she'd supposedly run away with, out of jealousy or something else. He could have tried to kill her, but something stopped him from making the blow fatal. Or maybe he'd run them off the road, she'd been knocked unconscious by the accident, and he'd quickly and efficiently killed his rival.

But why hadn't he finished her? Did he still want her? Or just her money?

He was stroking her, slowly, with erotic intent. His head dipped toward hers, blotting out the light. He was going to kiss her, she knew it. He had every right to kiss her—he was her husband.

So why did it feel as if it were going to be her first kiss?

She held herself very still, waiting for the touch of his mouth against hers, letting her eyes drift shut, aware of the danger, the draw of the man, and no longer caring if she was playing with fire.

And then he pulled back, abruptly. "That's enough questions for now, Molly," he said in a bored drawl. "This marital togetherness wears thin pretty damned fast. Go away."

She opened her eyes and stared at him in confusion. He wanted her. She knew that, with a sudden sureness that left her curiously triumphant. He wanted her, but he was half afraid of her.

It was a small consolation. He scared the hell out of her. She didn't bother arguing with him. She simply rose, taking her mug of undrinkable black sludge. "Pleasant dreams," she said sweetly.

His response was a growled obscenity. The dog lifted his head, looking at the two of them questioningly before lumbering to his feet, preparing to follow her.

"Beastie!" Patrick spoke sharply, and with an air of reluctance the dog returned to his side. Molly went slowly up the stairs, feeling oddly, doubly forsaken.

SHE LAY AWAKE for hours, listening to the rain beat down on the slate roof. The queen-size bed with its voluptuous satin sheets was too soft, and before an hour of tossing and turning had passed her back began to ache. The clinging nightgown, so revealing and provocative for a nonexistent lover, was obviously made to be discarded early in the night. It made her itch.

The room was stuffy and suffocating, and the

heavy formal drapes kept out any trace of moonlight. She lay there and hated that room, hated it with a passion. If she was going to be a prisoner there she would have to change it, despite her husband's likely objections. Surely he couldn't approve of the lavish style of it. How had he managed to put up with it when he used to visit his wife?

Or had she gone to his room?

She stiffened uncontrollably. Slow, measured footsteps were mounting the stairs, and she could hear the clicking of the dog's nails as he followed his master up to bed. She lay there, tense and unmoving, scarcely breathing, as she waited for him.

She hadn't imagined the look in his eyes earlier, the slow, sensual heat that he'd deliberately banked. He wanted her. And he seemed to be a man who took what he wanted.

He stopped in the hall, and she could almost hear his breathing. After a moment he went into his own room and closed the door.

She felt a stinging dampness in her eyes, and she wiped it away angrily. Molly Winters, who never cried, had wept three times in one day. She wasn't going to keep giving in to some maudlin weakness, she told herself firmly. She was glad he hadn't come to her room, that cool, angry stranger, she was absolutely delighted. As a matter of fact, the nurse had been right.

She hated Patrick Winters with his cold heart and his cold blue eyes, hated him more than she had hated any person in her entire life. She knew that hurt and hatred—it was a familiar companion in the old stone house.

PATRICK WASN'T QUITE SURE how he was going to stand this. He told himself there was no way he could hear her breathing through the thick old walls, no way he could smell the faint trace of perfume that clung to her hair.

But he could. The scent, the sound, the feel of her followed him into his bedroom, teased him unmercifully. The last few weeks had been the first peace he'd known in more than a year. He hadn't wanted her back, and he didn't want her sleeping two doors away from him, totally immune to him.

He wanted to be immune to her. Oblivious. To be able to ignore her, and the way she crawled beneath his skin, danced in his blood. His feelings for her should have been over long ago. They were never very sensible—she was a decade younger than he was, a sixteen-year-old child when he'd first seen her, a twenty-three-year-old child when he'd made the very dire mistake of marrying her.

And he couldn't blame anyone but himself. Sure, his damned autocratic father had set things in motion, determined to get his way, even beyond the grave. But Patrick had never danced to his tune. And marrying Jared Winters's chosen one should have been the last thing he'd do.

But the problem was damnably simple. His father had always known him far too well, for all they'd fought like cats and dogs. He'd chosen Molly for

him, for the simple reason that he knew Patrick
wanted her. Wanted her desperately.

Well, he'd gotten her. And desperation as well.
He'd made his bed, and he'd lie in it alone. Until
Molly was out of his house, out of his life, for good.

And then, maybe he'd be able to get her out of
his soul as well.

Chapter Four

The room was dark and still when she awoke the next morning, alone in the wide, uncomfortable bed. She was sweating all over, and her hands were trembling. Shaking herself slightly, she rolled out of bed. A nightmare, she told herself, as she pushed open the heavy drapes and stared out into the early Pennsylvania morning. The sky was a sullen blue, not unlike Patrick's eyes, and she felt as weighted down as the weather. She pushed open the window, hoping for a soft breeze, but she was rewarded with an icy blast of cold. She slammed it shut quickly.

The tiny gilt clock beside the massive bed said six-thirty, and she wondered whether she usually rose at such an early hour. She was in no mood to tempt fate with another nightmare—besides, she had too much she needed to learn. Maybe today was the day she'd begin to find out the answers to some of the thousands of questions plaguing her.

She went through the connecting door to the tiny bathroom and scrubbed at her face fiercely with hot water and the designer soap in the gold soap dish.

Looking into the mirror, she wondered once again
at the oddness of her surroundings: the cold, modern
luxury everywhere in her rooms. A luxury that was
both unnatural and stifling. But the reflection of that
long oval face with the slanted green-blue eyes was
that of a stranger, and could give her no answers.

She dressed swiftly in the same clothes she'd
worn the night before—from what she'd seen of the
overstuffed contents of the closet and dresser there
was nothing else even remotely suitable for an early
spring day on a farm. Though Molly had the feeling
this was no ordinary farm.

The old kitchen was even more attractive in day-
light. An old-fashioned brick hearth and oven took
up one wall, and a small fire was crackling cheerfully, bringing a warmth to the room that was spir-
itual as well as physical. The gleaming wooden
counter, the copper pots hanging from the white-
washed walls, the massive old cookstove and the
harvest table created a feeling of simple needs and
pleasures, and she found herself slightly, danger-
ously at peace for the first time since she'd arrived
in Bucks County. For the first time since she'd
woken up in that hospital room, just one short day
ago.

"My goodness, Mrs. Winters, what in the world
are you doing up so early?" an amazed voice demanded from the pantry door. "I was planning on
bringing you your breakfast in bed, same as I always
did." A starched, comfortable figure stood in the
doorway, another unnerving sign of normalcy.

"Good morning," Molly greeted her hesitantly,

taking in the woman's graying hair, curious black eyes and general air of motherliness. "I decided it was too nice a day to stay in bed."

The woman turned to peer out the window, then looked back at Molly in surprise. "Well, it's not exactly the day I'd pick for a picnic, but it's well enough, I suppose, especially after last night. And of course, you so long in the hospital, poor girl. Now you go and sit yourself down in the dining room and I'll set you a place in two shakes."

"If you don't mind I'd rather eat in here."

She looked even more startled. "Well, certainly, if that's what you want. I will admit it's warmer and cozier in here. Pat always eats his breakfast in here with me, and that's a fact. Says it warms him up." She kept a steady flow of chatter while she deftly set a place at the table, poured her a cup of coffee with just the right amount of cream and sugar, and started some toast. "What'll you have for breakfast, Mrs. Winters? The usual?"

Molly could feel an odd blush of color rise to her cheeks. "I'm afraid I...that is..."

"Oh, heavens, what a fool I am, jabbering away at you. Pat explained your little problem, but I forgot all about it. You probably don't even know who I am, do you? I'm Fran Morse, the housekeeper, and you usually have two slices of toast and orange juice. But maybe I could tempt you with something a bit more substantial this morning?"

Molly sipped at the wonderful coffee. "Well, my...Patrick made dinner last night," she said carefully, oddly unwilling to call Patrick her husband.

"Then you must be starving," the woman said with a friendly smile. "That man can't cook to save his life."

"I *am* a bit hungry," she admitted. "I'd love some eggs and bacon if it's not too much trouble. And some of your poppy seed muffins."

The woman beamed fondly. "Well, it's a treat to see you've got some appetite. These last few months you were eating like a bird. And you remembered my muffins, bless your heart!" She deposited some in front of Molly, kindly ignoring her sudden start.

She'd have to get used to remembering, Molly told herself shakily. Things are bound to come back like that, a bit at a time. She took a bite out of the muffin, and the familiar-unfamiliar taste warmed her tongue. Slowly she began to relax. For the first time since she arrived she felt comfortable and comparatively happy. Here was one person who didn't seem to blame her for a thousand anonymous crimes. Molly watched Mrs. Morse bustle around the kitchen with a sense of quiet gratitude, and she wished that feeling could last forever.

By the time she devoured her breakfast and had seconds of muffins and coffee she was ready to face the day. "Would you like some help washing up?" she offered, bringing her dishes over to the sink.

Mrs. Morse stared at her strangely. "Well, I never thought to hear such words from your mouth again," she said frankly. "But there, I always said you weren't so bad underneath. No, dearie, I can manage these myself. After all, it's what I'm paid for."

Molly nodded, trying to ignore those words that kept repeating themselves, around and around in her brain. *I always said you weren't so bad underneath.* Who did she say it to?

There wasn't much she could say in response. She plastered a cool smile on her face. "Well, if you need any help with lunch or anything just call me."

It was just past seven o'clock when she wandered out of the kitchen, more troubled than she cared to admit. She didn't know where to start. Her life was an Agatha Christie novel—full of clues and question marks, suspects and red herrings, and the thought of sorting them out was daunting. It didn't sound as if there was anyone she could turn to for help or answers—from the impression she'd gotten from Patrick and company she had no friends in the area, and it was unlikely that anyone would want to have anything to do with her.

She ended up back in the opulent bedroom, staring at the walls. Patrick had gotten up and left early, Willy apparently didn't make an appearance until past noon if he could help it, and Molly was doomed to her own frustrating company.

She went to the closet, looking through her wardrobe. Within minutes her disgust was even stronger. Those expensive clothes were absolutely lovely, but they were as ill-suited for her as gold lamé on a child. She went out on the landing and called to Mrs. Morse.

"Have we got an old trunk anywhere?"

"What in the world are you doing, Mrs. Win-

ters?'' She appeared at the bottom of the stairs, a
dust rag in one capable hand.

"Cleaning house, just like you," she replied
smartly. "Have we got a trunk anywhere?"

"Should be one in the back of your closet," Mrs.
Morse answered, curiosity alight in her face. "Do
you need any help?"

"I can handle it," she said, heading back in to
discover an old-fashioned steamer trunk, large
enough to hold even Molly Winters's extensive
wardrobe. Working at a leisurely pace, she loaded
it with almost every conceivable piece of elegant
clothing. Patrick must have been using understate-
ment when he said she loved to spend money. It
was a good thing she apparently had plenty of it.
The stuff in the closets and drawers must have cost
a fortune. Sudden guilt swamped her. Surely there
was some deserving charity in town that would love
something a bit better than rags.

She kept very little: a number of subdued cotton
sweaters, a blessed second pair of worn jeans. Out
went the gold-threaded caftan, the black satin sheath
with the neckline down to there, the turquoise silk
lounging pajamas. Whether she liked it or not, she
was really a T-shirt and jeans type, and dressing up
in sophisticated clothes would only make her look
more ridiculous. And make the situation that much
worse.

What situation? she asked herself suddenly. There
was no answer. Only the instinctive knowledge that
she wanted to be beautiful. Was she fool enough to
care what her bad-tempered husband thought? If she

harbored any warm emotions in that direction she would be wise to forget them quickly. Her life was a tangled mess, and she had absolutely no idea how things had gotten that way. She sighed as she shut the trunk on the expensive, unsuitable clothes.

There wasn't much left. Several drawers full of lace underwear that she'd lost her heart to, those itchy nightgowns, and the sweaters and shirts. And one very beautiful eyelet and cotton dress of pure white. The woman Molly had begun to think of as her predecessor didn't seem to go in for simple things like this, and she wondered if it had actually belonged to someone else. For the time being she could wear it if the occasion demanded a dress, which seemed unlikely. From what Patrick had said, it seemed as if she were to be kept in total seclusion. Until her memory returned, Molly thought she might prefer it that way.

She glanced down at her clothes. Sooner or later she would find out how to get hold of her money. She'd need to buy at least a few new things—she couldn't spend all her time in two pairs of faded jeans and a few sweaters. Then again, maybe she could. After all, who was she trying to impress? If it was Patrick Winters, it was obviously a lost cause.

"I'VE GOT A TRUNK full of clothes up there." Molly walked into the kitchen. "Have you any idea where I could send it?"

Mrs. Morse looked up from her luncheon fixings in surprise. "Send it?" she repeated blankly.

"Yes." Molly reached out and snatched a piece

of sliced carrot. "I don't want them anymore. They're not at all my style."

"I was wondering if you'd ever learn that." She offered her another carrot. "I'll have Ben take care of it for you when he comes in for lunch."

"Ben?"

She looked at her oddly. "My husband," she said after an uncomfortable silence. "You've only known him since you were sixteen."

Molly shrugged with embarrassment. "Will lunch be ready soon? I'm starving."

She nodded, an even more uncomfortable look passing over her face. "Mrs. Winters, I don't know if it's my place to say this, but..."

"Have you always called me Mrs. Winters?" Molly interrupted, snatching one more carrot.

"Since you've been married. Before that you were Molly to me and Ben."

"Then I think I should be Molly again." She smiled warmly at her. "Mrs. Winters doesn't seem like me at all. Molly at least seems a little closer to who I feel like."

"All right. If that's what you want." She glanced uneasily toward the door. "I think I'd better tell you something before they come in for lunch."

It was there, a tiny fluttering of anxiety in the pit of her stomach. She managed a calm smile. "Tell me what, Mrs. Morse?" She leaned against the counter, hoping she looked nonchalant.

"It's common knowledge around here that they're going to be married as soon as the divorce is final."

She said it all in a rush, clearly eager to get it over with.

Molly looked at her blankly. "Who's going to marry whom?"

"Patrick. It looks like he's going to marry Mrs. Canning. Her husband passed away the day you left here and it looked like they started making their plans right away." She looked miserable. "I thought you'd better know, in case you started getting... well, getting ideas."

"What kind of ideas would those be? That my husband shouldn't be getting ready for wife number two before he's gotten rid of wife number one?" She couldn't keep the trace of bitterness out of her voice. "Who's Mrs. Canning? Do I know her?"

"You and Lisa Canning used to be thick as thieves," Mrs. Morse replied grimly. "She and Patrick are out riding now. I'm expecting them in for lunch any minute now. If you want I can give you a tray in your room. It couldn't be very pleasant for you, dearie. It's always been that way between Patrick and her, ever since she married old Fred Canning and moved here five years ago. Though I used to think it was more on her side than his."

"Then why did he marry me? For the money? He told me I was rich."

"I was never really sure of why he married you, honey. I guess I hoped that he loved you."

"But he didn't. Did he?"

She wouldn't answer, busying herself with the dishes. Then she looked up. "All I know is that Pat wouldn't have done something like that. If he'd wanted that money there were other ways he could have gotten it.''

Like killing me, she thought, unable to hide from the chilling notion.

At that moment there was a commotion in the yard, and with a false calm Molly moved to the window and looked out. And some of the pieces fell together in the puzzle.

At first her attention was drawn to the man who was still, ostensibly, her husband. He looked as if he were born in the saddle. He was tall and gorgeous in the bright sunlight, his long, muscled legs easily controlling the spirited bay, and Molly had no doubts at all as to why she had married him. By his side was her erstwhile friend Mrs. Canning, a well-preserved beauty of indeterminate age, her white blond hair expertly tinted and coiffed, her face youthful, her figure opulent and desirable. Everything Molly was not. She laughed and put one hand on Patrick's arm, and the look he gave her was one that sent such a flashing wave of jealousy through Molly that she felt sick. She might not remember Patrick or the woman, but that emotion was an old and comfortable foe.

The woman dismounted from the horse in one lithe movement, and suddenly Molly realized why she looked vaguely familiar. She belonged in that bedroom upstairs, with the pink-tinted satins, in those sophisticated and expensive clothes. They were made for a woman like her, and Molly wondered who had decorated that bedroom and chosen those clothes. Had it been Patrick? Or the helpful

Mrs. Canning? Or had Molly tried to turn herself into a clone of the woman Patrick loved?

They were already seated when she walked into the dining room. "Molly, darling!" Mrs. Canning rose and enveloped her in a warm and highly scented embrace. Poison, Molly decided, a fitting enough scent, and then cursed herself for knowing the names of perfumes and not of her closest friends.

"We missed you so much," the woman continued, her heavy gold bangles digging into Molly's back. She drew away and looked into her face, frowning. "You don't look at all well, my dear. And where did you get those awful clothes?"

"From my room," she answered lightly, drawing away as unobtrusively as she could manage. "It's good to see you again."

Her luminous eyes were warm and friendly and just ever so slightly assessing. "Darling, it's so good to see *you!* We were paralyzed when you ran off like that, absolutely paralyzed." She moved back to the table and put one possessive hand on Patrick's arm. "Weren't we, darling?"

Molly half expected to see painted fingernails like red claws. Wasn't the Other Woman always supposed to have red fingernails? The hand on Patrick's forearm was well-shaped, with pale, well-manicured nails. And not nearly as interesting as the tanned, muscular forearm beneath it, Molly thought hopelessly.

Patrick had risen. He simply looked at her, an unwelcoming expression on his face. Molly thought of her room with a faint trace of longing, then steeled herself.

He didn't look like a man who could kill. He simply looked like a man surrounded by too many women.

Another motive, though. If Molly died, Patrick would have her money and revenge for her running away with another man. He'd also have the beautiful Mrs. Canning, and Molly had to admit that most men would have found that incentive indeed.

"Wouldn't you rather have a tray in your room, Molly?" he asked in a cool voice. "You've just gotten out of the hospital, and you look tired."

"Heavens, no!" she said so brightly she wanted to wince. "I need to get back in the swing of things. I need to spend time with friends and family. Loved ones," she added with a pointed, saccharine look at Patrick.

She might have pushed him too far. He shoved back from the table, but once more Lisa put a restraining hand on his arm, and he subsided with a glare in Molly's direction.

"Pat says you have amnesia," Lisa murmured. "How fascinating. It sounds like something out of a bad novel."

"It is," Patrick growled.

"I'm surprised he told you," Molly said, ignoring him. "I get the impression that my husband doesn't quite believe me."

His response was a disbelieving snort. Lisa's hand tightened warningly on his arm, and Molly couldn't tear her gaze away from that possessive clasp.

"Of course he believes you, Molly. Why else would you have run off without a word to me, your dearest friend? Or to your husband, or anyone? You must have had a reason, and if you could only remember I'm sure you'd tell us everything."

Molly looked at them both. The dearest friend, with her phony, cooing concern and her possessive grip. The husband, watching her with stony distrust.

They could have been in it together, Molly thought. Her disappearance benefited everyone. It was no wonder she'd run.

"Of course," she said calmly, helping herself to the plate of delicate sandwiches Mrs. Morse had provided. She was famished, and she didn't care if her abstemious so-called friend watched as she devoured her lunch.

Molly shoved a sandwich into her mouth, then reached for another. "So tell me," she said in a conversational voice, "what's been happening with you two while I've been away?"

Patrick promptly choked on his coffee.

IT HAD BEEN an illuminating meal, Molly thought several hours later as she sat cross-legged on her bed, staring down at the telltale handkerchief. Lisa was obviously adept at awkward social situations, Patrick had been totally uninterested in putting a smooth front on anything. Clearly everyone knew about Lisa and Patrick—just as clearly, it was supposed to be ignored.

Molly played the game very well. She made all the right responses, slipping easily into the role of younger friend. So easily that she suspected that was how it used to be with the three of them.

Lisa and Patrick, tolerant of the exuberant teenager who followed them around. She could almost see it, almost remember it.

Why hadn't he married Lisa? Belatedly, she remembered Lisa's elderly husband. Mrs. Morse said he'd died recently, yet Lisa hardly seemed the grieving widow. It was too bad the old man hadn't died ten months ago and saved everyone a great deal of trouble. Patrick could have married Lisa instead of settling for his wealthy fifth cousin twice removed or whatever she was.

She stared down at the scrap of cloth in her hand. Those orange streaks looked oddly familiar, yet she couldn't trace them. They were neither rust nor blood stains, and she wondered why the police hadn't taken it for evidence. Had she hidden it from them? If so, why?

So many questions. She was still hungry, and she was exhausted. Patrick had left the table abruptly, Lisa vanished soon after, and Molly could only imagine where they were and what they were doing.

She didn't want to.

She lay back on her bed, tucking the handkerchief beneath her pillow. She wasn't ready to have anyone see it. She wasn't certain what it signified, but right now it was the only clue, the only advantage she had. She wasn't about to let anyone else get a look at it until she was good and ready.

Chapter Five

Amnesia. What a crock! Who did Molly think she was, expecting them to believe such a cock-and-bull story? Maybe in romance novels, maybe in TV movies, but not in real life.

It was just a little too damned convenient. As long as she pretended not to remember anything, she was buying herself time.

But she couldn't keep it up forever. Sure, her eyes looked wide and guileless as she looked at each of them in turn, but she could be acting. She'd gotten damned good at it.

If she wasn't faking, then things were even more dangerous. If that too convenient amnesia was the real McCoy, it could disappear as quickly as it came. Leaving her with a clear memory of what had happened to her just a few short weeks ago.

And what had happened to the man known as George Andrews.

That couldn't be allowed to happen. She was going to have to die. Sooner or later.

And sooner would be a much more acceptable alternative.

MOLLY WOKE UP in darkness, disoriented, panicked. It took her a moment to remember where she was. She sat up in bed, switching on the light, trying to still the fear that washed over her. She was just feeling stir crazy—she hadn't wanted to go outside for fear she'd run into Patrick and Lisa. An hour of their company had been about all she could handle. She knew she wouldn't be allowed to take the car anywhere until she'd proven her *trustworthiness* to that self-righteous, adulterous pig of a husband, even though the car might very well belong to her. Willy had disappeared as soon as he got up, and she didn't even have his doubtful company to distract her. There was a stack of mysteries in the bookcase, but to her disgust once more her memory failed her. She may not have known her own face, name, or even how she drank her coffee, but all she had to do was read the opening paragraph to remember whodunit.

She still hadn't met the other occupant of the old stone farmhouse. Cousin Ermintrude White, known to her as Aunt Ermy, said Mrs. Morse, was off on one of her incessant rounds of visits. Molly could tell from the housekeeper's look of disdain that Ermintrude White was not looked upon with affection in this household. Indeed, most of Mrs. Morse's approval seemed reserved for Patrick, despite his lapse in taste when it came to Mrs. Canning, and for Molly, a fact which surprised her. Here was one person who didn't hold her previous bad behavior against her. Perhaps if one dug deep enough there were excuses, but at that point Molly couldn't begin to fathom what they could be.

Nor was she particularly interested in hearing the details of all the evil she had done, at least, not from the one person who seemed to like her. Molly was simply glad to bask in the sudden affection. She was a good woman, Mrs. Morse, and it felt oddly encouraging to have her approval.

She heard the heavy footsteps first, followed by the peremptory knocking on her door. She leaned back, waiting, knowing perfectly well who was coming upstairs in such a towering rage. She had no intention of reacting if she could help it.

The door flew open and Patrick stood there, tall and lean against the doorway, and for a moment she felt a little clutching sense of longing. One that disappeared when she realized this wasn't a friendly visit.

"I would have thought," he said, his voice cold and cutting, "that you would have the common courtesy to abide by the schedule in this house. I should have known it would be too much to ask, but nevertheless I not only ask it, I demand it. You will come downstairs for drinks right now and be polite to our guests. I suppose even you are capable of that much." The withering contempt cut through her as she lay there motionless. "Now!" He moved into the room menacingly, and she sprang from the bed before she could stop herself.

He laughed then, and it wasn't a pleasant sound. "I'm glad to see I'm at least able to frighten you

into decent behavior. We'll be in the library.'' He
started out the door, stopped and turned. ''By the
way, in case you've forgotten, you usually dress for
dinner.''

Molly could see from the faint light in the hall
that he was still wearing his faded jeans, and she
shrugged with a fine show of bravado. ''I have no
clothes,'' she said simply. ''These will have to do.''

''By that I assume you mean that your extrava-
gant wardrobe no longer interests you and you wish
to go out and spend a similar sum or more.'' He
shrugged. ''Be my guest. Mrs. Morse can accom-
pany you if you insist. After all, it's your money.''

''How much money is there?'' she demanded,
scrambling off the bed.

''I wondered when you'd get around to asking,''
he said with an unpleasant laugh. ''As a matter of
fact, it was your seeming disinterest in money that
almost had me believing your cock-and-bull story
about amnesia. I should have known you couldn't
keep it up.''

''I merely wanted to know,'' she said in a cool
voice, ''if I have enough to buy you off. If I give it
to you would you let me go?''

She'd managed to startle him. ''I don't want your
damned money,'' he said bitterly.

''Then what do you want from me? Why did you
marry me?'' She scrambled off the bed, starting toward him. She was deliberately trying to goad him,
and she told herself she was simply wanting to get
the truth from him. And she knew she was lying.

She was trying to goad him into touching her

again. She wanted to see if his touch still made her tremble, as it had last night.

He backed away, not bothering to hide his uneasiness. "Be down in five minutes, Molly. Or I'll come back to get you."

It was supposed to be a threat. It sounded more like a temptation to Molly.

She waited just long enough before leaving the room, running down the curving stairs swiftly, two at a time, knowing if she hesitated she would lose her courage. Stopping before the living room door, she heard the noise of glasses and ice, quiet laughter and camaraderie that would vanish the moment she appeared. But appear she must—her husband had so decreed. Taking a deep breath, she ambled into the room with studied unconcern.

Patrick ignored her when she entered the room, busying himself at the bar.

"There you are, darling!" Lisa greeted her. She was curled up on the sofa like a contented cat. "Did you have a nice afternoon?"

"Lovely," she replied politely. "And you?"

Lisa cast a meaningful glance at Patrick's back, and her smile was unbearably smug. "Very stimulating."

Molly gritted her teeth, glancing around the room to see Willy, who seemed to be viewing the proceedings with a great deal of faintly drunken amusement.

"How are you tonight, Willy?" she greeted him, desperate to remove herself from Lisa's arch glances. She didn't need her far from subtle reminder of what she'd been doing with Molly's husband.

"Good enough, m'dear," Willy answered, raising a dark amber drink in greeting. "Glad to see you decided to join us after all."

She felt a sudden spurt of anger at all of them. They must have discussed poor little Molly in their various condescending tones, conspiring to torment and embarrass her. Well, she wouldn't let them down, she decided suddenly, throwing herself down into the most comfortable chair in the room and glowering at them all like a spoiled teenager.

Patrick stalked over to her to thrust a tall glass of bright red liquid at her. "Here you are," he said with false solicitude, and she controlled the urge to throw the drink back in his face.

"What is it?" she demanded suspiciously.

He raised an eyebrow. "Your usual. Cranberry juice, just as Aunt Ermy ordered for you, though tonight without the vodka. I assume you aren't allowed to drink after your supposed blow on the head." His voice was cool and disbelieving, and she barely controlled an equally snappish answer.

Instead she took a small, ladylike sip of it and wondered absently if among her myriad other faults she had been a drunk as well. She took a second, larger sip and leaned back further into the protective recesses of the chair to watch her family and friends.

Her participation was not missed. Willy, Patrick and Lisa were deeply involved in a discussion of horse breeding, a subject as foreign to her as mountain climbing. Though of course, she thought ruefully, she could very well have dabbled in both. She was the first one to notice the arrival of another guest, walking quietly along the stone-floored hallway. He was above medium height, though shorter than the lanky Patrick, with curly brown hair and a quiet intensity about his eyes. He looked handsome, shy, and out of place, and quite friendly in a quiet, gentle way, so far removed from the tightly leashed violence she sensed in her husband. She suddenly felt a little more optimistic. Maybe she'd finally found an ally among all these enemies.

"Hello, there." He cleared his throat at the door and they turned to greet him with enthusiasm.

"Toby!" Patrick's sudden, friendly grin was a revelation. "We were just discussing Arab's points. We'll forgive you for being late if you can clear something up."

Molly stared at Patrick, shocked into momentary silence. Remembering, almost remembering, with the sight of that sudden, devastating smile...

And then Toby stepped between them, and his eyes were warm and sympathetic. "How are you, Molly? We missed you."

The others were staring at him with silent disapproval, as if they suddenly discovered they had a traitor in their midst, but Toby didn't seem to notice. For the first time someone seemed sincerely glad to have her back, and Molly's eyes threatened to fill with those unwanted tears again.

"Thank you, Toby," she said softly, smiling up at him.

"Let's go in to dinner," Patrick said abruptly,

breaking the moment. He took Lisa's silk-clad arm and led her toward the dining room. "I could eat a horse. Next time I invite you for dinner you come on time, boy," he said with mock seriousness, and Toby laughed.

"I was held up, Pat," he said, following Willy's beefy form. "Miss Molly's just about to foal and I didn't know whether I dared come at all."

By the time Molly entered the dining room she noticed with a grimace that Lisa had taken the traditional seat for the woman of the household, at the foot of the table opposite Patrick, and she was relegated to a seat next to Willy. She sank down with sullen grace, wondering once more what she could have possibly done to have turned her family and friends against her. And what further insults would she have to bear while she remained a prisoner in this house. At least there was Toby, looking across at her with undisguised admiration. She tried to concentrate on that, shutting out the sound of Lisa's arch laughter as she flirted with Patrick.

"Molly, darling." Lisa turned to her in a coaxing voice. "Pat says you want to do some clothes shopping. I'd be delighted to come with you, give you a few pointers on style." Her expression told Molly that she badly needed all the help she could get.

"No, thank you, Lisa." She managed to control the faintly homicidal urge that was building up in her. "Mrs. Morse will come with me—I wouldn't think of bothering you."

"But darling, it's no bother," she protested prettily. "Remember what fun we had, picking all your other clothes? I've always helped you choose; you know I love to do it.''

So she had Lisa to thank for that closet full of unsuitable clothes, Molly thought. *And I bet she did it on purpose.* "No, I don't think so, Lisa. I prefer to choose my own clothes." Her voice was cool and firm, and there was nothing Lisa could do but shrug her elegant shoulders and exchange a look with Patrick as if to say, what can I do?

Toby tried to smooth over the moment of tension by expressing a sudden interest in the weather, but Molly had finally had enough of the strained atmosphere and subtle sniping. Of the secrets that no one was supposed to mention. "Tell me, Lisa," she said in a casual voice, flashing her as false a smile as she'd been given. "When is it that you and Patrick plan to marry?"

"I beg your pardon?" Lisa demanded in frosty tones.

Molly took a bite out of the rich chocolate cake Mrs. Morse had provided for dessert, revelling in the shocked expressions of all those around the table. She looked up with innocent eyes. "I just thought it would be easier if I knew what your schedule was. Your husband's been dead...how long? I think I was told it was five weeks, is that right? And I gather you've both been planning this for years, so I'd hate to make you drag out any role-playing as a grieving widow." Molly's eyes drifted down Lisa's seductive apparel with a faint smile. "Perhaps you could persuade my husband to get an apartment somewhere while we wait for the divorce to go through. I wouldn't want to cramp your style, and you *are* so good at persuading my husband.''

''Get out of here,'' Patrick said quietly. Molly turned her blandly innocent smile in his direction, wanting to lash out and hurt him.

''But why are you so mad, darling?'' She mimicked Lisa's tone of voice perfectly. ''You shouldn't let the fact that her husband's barely cold in the ground get in the way of your plans. After all, you only married me because you couldn't have her. And now you've got her. Happy happy, joy joy.'' She rose and stalked out of the room, anger finally taking control. She was halfway up the stairs when she heard him coming after her. Stifling a sudden, panic-stricken desire to run and lock herself in that sybaritic room, she turned at the top of the stairs and waited for him with spurious calm.

He caught her wrist in a grip that was almost painful, his blue eyes dark with anger. ''What the hell did you mean by that little scene in there?'' he demanded.

''Isn't it true?'' she asked quietly. ''Isn't every word I said true?''

''You have no right to criticize anybody. Not when you're dealing with gossip and suppositions and half-truths,'' he said in a furious undertone. ''I didn't run off in the middle of the night, I didn't set fire to the east barn and kill three horses, I didn't crack old Ben on the head and leave him bleeding in the middle of the yard. I wasn't found unconscious with a murdered man beside me.''

Molly felt sick and shaken. "And you're saying I did these things?" she asked in a hoarse whisper.

His voice came towards her, cold and distant with what she now knew was a justifiable rage. "No one else could have. Either you or the man you ran away with. Half our breeding stock went in that fire. Have you ever seen a barn fire, Molly? Do you know what it's like, listening to the screams of the horses, smelling the charred flesh, knowing there's nothing you can do to save them?"

She shook her head and tried to pull away, but he was inexorable.

"The house nearly went too. Did you know that? Not that you'd care. You're just a spoiled, vicious child who lashes out and destroys without thinking when she doesn't get her own way!"

"And what was my own way?" she demanded, fighting to hold on to her self-control.

He shook his head in disgust. "You never told me," he said, quiet now. "Stay out of my path, Molly. If you come down for dinner again you'd better by God be polite or I swear I'll break your pretty little neck."

She stood alone on the landing, unmoving, for long minutes after he'd left her to return to his guests. She glanced down at her hand as it rested on the railing, and she realized she was clutching it tightly.

He said she'd hit Ben Morse over the head and left him bleeding. Surely Mrs. Morse couldn't believe her capable of such a thing and still be as friendly to her? Not everyone believed her to be such a monster, including one of the people she'd supposedly hurt the most.

Damn Patrick and his accusations, accusations she couldn't refute. She stared after him, shaking with fury and defiance, when a stray thought entered her mind. A pretty little neck, he'd said. One he wanted to break.

Had he been the one? Had he driven her from this place, then followed her, murdered the man she was with and then bashed her over the head, hoping to have killed her?

And if he had, what was to stop him from trying it again?

Why did he want her there? Why couldn't he just let her leave, start a new life with the faint shreds of her memory? What in God's name did he want from her?

And what did she want from him?

Chapter Six

The sickness started the next morning. She woke up at the crack of dawn, a sudden churning in her stomach. She barely made it to the bathroom in time before she was thoroughly and violently sick. And as soon as the first spasm passed a second one came on, and then a third.

When it finally passed she was weak and shaken, and it took every last remaining ounce of energy to crawl back into bed and lie there, shivering. She had never felt so horribly, desperately ill in her entire life, and she wondered whether it could have been food poisoning. With her current run of luck it could have descended on her and left the others, including Lisa Canning, in perfect health.

She was just being paranoid—Mrs. Morse seemed like a careful and excellent cook. No, it must be some virus, brought on by her recent hospitalization. Maybe just an accumulation of stress. It would pass soon enough.

It was almost an hour before she felt able to climb out of bed, and she took a long, slow time to get dressed and washed and make her shaky way downstairs. Mrs. Morse took one look at her and clucked sympathetically.

"You don't look at all well, Molly, my dear," she said as she hustled her over to the seat by the blazing fire and wrapped an afghan around her. "It's not a fit day out for man nor beast, so it's just as well. Patrick said you wanted to go shopping but I think we'd better put it off for the time being. I'll make you some mint tea with honey and see how that makes you feel." She clucked over her like a mother hen, and Molly slowly began to relax. It was a rare, comfortable feeling, being cared for and fussed over, especially after Patrick's accusations of the night before.

"It's just some sort of stomach virus," she said nonchalantly. "I'm already feeling better—I'd like to go shopping, really!" She felt like a child begging for a treat. The thought of spending another day cooped up in that house with its atmosphere of brooding guilt was enough to make her desperate.

"We'll see," Mrs. Morse said, bustling around. "I'm going to make you some nice, nourishing oatmeal and then we'll see how you feel. Nothing like oatmeal for an upset stomach!"

THREE HOURS LATER they were on the road, and whether it was from oatmeal, natural causes or sheer willpower, Molly was feeling fine.

"All right, all right," Mrs. Morse had finally acquiesced. "Patrick and Ben won't be in to lunch today—they're busy down at the lower barn. So we might as well take off right now. You'll have to give me a hand with dinner, mind you, if I'm to spend the afternoon gallivanting around."

At the sound of Ben's name she paused, suddenly stricken. "Mrs. Morse?" she said in a hesitant voice.

"What is it, lovey?"

"Do you believe I did what they say I did? Do you think I hit your husband over the head and left him bleeding on the ground?" She held her breath, half afraid of the answer.

Mrs. Morse shook her head. "You've been accused of a lot of things this past year. Some of them you told me about yourself, bragging. But I can't believe you would have changed so much you would have hurt my Ben. Neither does he. He doesn't know who sneaked up behind him and hit him over the head, but he knows it wasn't you."

"Thank God," Molly breathed. "But who could it have been? Were there any strangers around here?"

"Just the man you ran away with."

The words hung in the air between them. "So I am responsible," she said in a low voice.

"No, dearie. You got in with a bad crowd. You were unhappy, and you didn't use your best judgment. But that's in the past. Ben doesn't hold a grudge, and neither do I."

Molly looked at her, stricken. "I'll find out what really happened," she said. "Sooner or later I'll remember."

"Of course you will, dearie. In the meantime, we

have some shopping to do. Nothing like a little shopping to cheer a body up."

Molly rose, some of her earlier enthusiasm vanished. "I forgot. How am I going to get money?"

"What do you need money for, with all those credit cards?" Mrs. Morse demanded. "Besides, I wouldn't be surprised if you had money in your wallet. You always forget that you have any."

"I don't know where my wallet is," she admitted.

Mrs. Morse had the grace to look abashed. "That's right—Patrick has it in the office. Since he told me it was all right to take you shopping I'm sure he'd expect me to give it to you. You just wait a moment and I'll go fetch it."

Molly had grave doubts where Patrick had any such expectations, but she accepted the calfskin wallet with carefully concealed gratitude. Mrs. Morse was right about the credit cards and the money. If she wanted to escape from there she wouldn't have to worry about finances. She had it all in her hand, along with her driver's license.

Putting the wallet in the hip pocket of her jeans, she strode out of the room. Right then she had no intention of leaving. Not with so many questions left unanswered. Why didn't anyone know who George Andrews was? Why didn't they know for sure who hit Ben? Who killed the man in the car with her? And why in God's name was all this happening?

She was going to find out the truth if it killed her. And she had another motive as well. Lisa Canning wasn't going to have her way without a fight. Molly had every intention of staying long enough to put a stop to that relationship, finalize the divorce, and then be on her merry little way.

Somehow the idea didn't warm her in the slightest.

THE DAY IN NEW HOPE was a complete success. They had lunch in an elegant little French restaurant just opened for the season, dining sumptuously on the rich French food despite Mrs. Morse's warning glance. And then they went on a buying spree, jeans and khakis, cotton sweaters and denim shirts, leather boots, a tweed jacket, flannel nightgowns and running shoes. Mrs. Morse looked scandalized at her extravagance in an amused sort of way, and when Molly finally finished she contented herself with the comment that she didn't do things by half measures.

"Though I must say, Molly, that these clothes are much better suited to you than the ones that Mrs. Canning had you buy. I just hope you don't go through these as fast."

"I don't plan to," she said from over the tower of packages that surrounded them in the front seat and completely filled the back of the van. "I expect these will last me for a long, long time."

"Well, that's nice. And Patrick will just love the sweater you bought for him, I know he will."

Once more Molly was filled with misgivings. "Do you really think so?" she asked anxiously, her cheerfulness fading. The thick blue cotton sweater would match his cold eyes perfectly, and yet Molly doubted he had any desire to accept presents from her. Maybe she'd just put it away in a drawer until he had a birthday or something. Assuming she was going to be around for his birthday. Otherwise she could just give it to him as a divorce present. For some reason she doubted the thought would amuse him.

She was putting her new clothes away in the ugly dresser when a shadow fell across the doorway. She looked up, into the scowling face of her handsome husband.

"I thought you should have these while you're here," he said abruptly, tossing a small box onto the bed. "Despite your insistence that you'd never wear them, they *are* yours."

She knew what she'd find in that small, ivory box. Her wedding and engagement rings lay nestled against gray velvet. Neither of them struck any chord in her memory, the plain gold band nor the large sapphire in the old-fashioned setting. She slipped them on her ring finger, noting helplessly the perfect fit. Circumstances seemed determined to make her accept what her mind still found unacceptable. She was, it seemed, the selfish and spoiled wife of a brooding and very angry man. It was useless to waste any more time denying it.

She looked up at him, but there was no reading the expression on his face. "Why did I decide to take them off?" she asked. "Did I leave them behind when I left?"

"You never wore them."

He'd managed to shock her. "Why not?"

"You can cut the innocent surprise, Molly. You

know perfectly well you threw them back at me the morning after we were married.''

"You were that bad in bed?" she asked lightly.

He stared at her, an odd expression in his eyes. "You must have thought so," was all he said, turning on his heel to leave her.

She watched him go, wishing there was some way she could interpret that odd expression on his face. Another mystery, among too many mysteries.

She changed into a pair of khakis and a navy cotton sweater before making her way down to the kitchen. She was in the midst of peeling potatoes, temporarily alone in the vast, comfortable room, when Patrick reappeared. He looked at her, seemed about to beat a hasty retreat, and then obviously thought better of it. It appeared her husband was no more a coward than she was.

He moved into the room with that undeniable grace and leaned against the counter, a few feet away from her. "I see you decided to wear your rings," he said in that husky voice which she found so inexplicably attractive. Unfortunately she found everything about the man inexplicably attractive, from his lean, austere face to his long, muscular legs. Everything, that is, except his attitude toward his wife.

She nodded, concentrating fiercely on the potato in her hand. She felt suddenly nervous and tongue-tied with him so close, and she wondered whether that reticence was a normal part of her behavior.

Apparently not, she thought. "You've changed,"

he said suddenly, and she could feel those bright blue eyes on her, sense their puzzlement.

"Have I?" Her voice was carefully light. "I wouldn't know." She looked up at him with all the courage she could muster. "You know, I really don't remember what I was like before. I can't remember a thing."

"Maybe you can't," he said enigmatically, moving closer to the table. "Or else you're a damned good actress." He leaned across her, his body brushing against hers just slightly as he turned on the lamp. "But then, you always were good at covering things up."

The faint touch of his body against hers had almost sent the knife slicing through her hand, and it took all her self-control to hide her sudden agitation. *Why in God's name does he have such an effect on me?*

He leaned back, watching her out of solemn eyes. "It's good of you to help Mrs. Morse with dinner."

She nodded, tossing one potato into the bowl of water and picking up another. After a moment she felt him move away, and she breathed a tiny, imperceptible sigh of relief.

"Come in for drinks when you're finished," he said suddenly. "We may as well try to behave like reasonable adults as long as you're here."

As a graceful invitation it still lacked a lot, but Molly found herself suddenly hopeful.

"What are you looking so happy about all of a sudden, missy?" Mrs. Morse demanded of her as she bustled back into the kitchen. "You win the lottery or something?"

Molly shrugged, hiding her face. She knew perfectly well that her reaction to his slight mellowing was all out of proportion, but it didn't matter. She had learned one thing about her loss of memory that she didn't find very comforting.

She might have forgotten names and faces and people and events, but she hadn't forgotten emotions. She cared about her husband, quite desperately, and his feelings toward her were at best decidedly lukewarm, at times bordering on hatred. But his partial civility tonight was a start. She began humming a tuneless little hum.

"You'd better let me finish those," Mrs. Morse offered after a few minutes, "and go in and get yourself a drink. I can take care of the rest. Thanks for the help."

She wanted to go find Patrick. To test out this new, inexplicable feeling. She wanted to stay in the kitchen, hidden away like a latter-day Cinderella. She squared her shoulders. "Any time."

Patrick was sitting in front of the fire, a glass in his hand, staring thoughtfully into space. He frowned when he saw her, and she firmly controlled a strong desire to run back upstairs, away from his obvious disapproval. Instead she smiled shyly.

No reaction. Since he didn't seem about to move, she poured herself a glass of the cranberry juice that seemed reserved for her and went to a seat near the fire. Near him. His eyes were fastened on her now, and she wondered what he was thinking. Probably comparing her to Lisa, she thought, and she knew who would come out ahead in that little competition.

"Why did you marry me?" she asked quietly, tucking her feet up under her. "Was it only for the money?"

He jumped, and his drink splashed onto his jeans. "Why do you ask?" he countered gruffly.

"We weren't in love, were we?"

"No, not at all," he answered after a moment. Whether he thought she was lying about her memory or not, he'd obviously decided to give her the benefit of the doubt. For now. "It seemed like the logical thing to do at the time. It was what my father wanted, and you were always eager to please my father."

"Were you? Eager to please your father, that is?"

"No," he said flatly. "I spent most of my life going out of my way to drive him crazy. We were both too strong willed. He only had to decide something for me to take the opposite view."

"Then if your father thought we should get married, why did you give in?"

His smile was wintry cold in the dim light. "My father was more adept than most at getting his own way, even beyond the grave. He left his place to me, of course. I was his only child, his heir. But he left the majority of the money to you. Hadn't you wondered where it came from? Part of my father's twisted sense of humor. He knew I needed the money to keep this place going, and you needed a home. It seemed an obvious solution, and I decided to be practical for once. He was dead—there was no need to rebel against him anymore.''

Molly stared at him, appalled. ''Didn't I expect to fall in love at some point?'' she asked a bit breathlessly. ''Why in heaven's name would I agree to marry you?''

He shrugged. ''You didn't share your thoughts on the subject with me at the time. You always used to love this place—you said it was the only real home you'd ever known. And you loved my father. You wanted what he wanted.''

He leaned back, staring into the fire. ''He left the estate that way on purpose, you know. From the moment you came here he was determined that sooner or later we'd get married. Perfect blood lines, he'd decided, and once Father decided something there was no talking him out of it. He wanted to breed thoroughbred grandchildren the way he bred thoroughbred horses.''

''But we didn't.''

''Didn't what?'' he said in a rough voice.

''Breed perfect grandchildren.''

His laugh was short and mirthless. ''Neither of us were in the mood. Don't worry, Molly, we won't have to suffer much longer from our mistake, I can promise you that. As soon as the divorce comes through you can take all your money and leave.''

''And how will you support Winter's Edge?'' she asked. ''Or is your future wife rich enough to provide you with the capital you need? It must be convenient, finding wealthy women willing to marry and support you in the style to which you seem accustomed.'' Her voice was bitter with an old, forgotten hurt.

He turned on her savagely. "She is not my future wife, damn you. And it's none of your business how I support this place. I can manage without your help, without your money. If my father hadn't been so damned good at playing games it never would have been your money.'' He took a long pull on his drink.

"That was the only reason I married you?" she asked, unable to leave it alone. There was something more there, something he wasn't telling her.

He looked up, a faint, cynical expression in his eyes. "Well, there was the fact that you'd had a crush on me since you were sixteen. That may have had something to do with it.''

"I was in love with you?" she said in a hushed voice.

"No!" It was a sharp protest. "You were a lonely adolescent who thought I was the perfect romantic hero. You used to follow me around like a lost puppy dog.''

She could feel color flood her cheeks, and she bit her lip. This was her fault, she'd pushed him. But she wished he'd shown just a trace more compassion. "How very embarrassing for you," she said faintly. "I must have put quite a damper on your love life.''

"Not particularly," he said, and she couldn't be sure what he was referring to.

"And when did I get over this embarrassing infatuation?" she asked lightly.

He stared at her, cool and removed. "On our wedding day," he said flatly. "I'm getting sick of nostalgia, Molly. Either be quiet or go away."

She stared at him out of shadowed eyes, wondering whether throwing her drink at him might help. She retreated into silence, settling back against the cushions with every appearance of unconcern as she concentrated on the dancing flames in the fireplace. Even Beastie's presence by her side was more torment than comfort, reminding her how alone she was in this place.

She glanced across the room at Patrick, unable to help herself. He was as cold as ice, and she wondered whether spring would ever touch the inhabitants of the old stone house, or whether they'd remain forever trapped in the icy winter.

CONVERSATION AT DINNER that night was stilted. Uncle Willy was his usual slightly drunken self, and decided to make up for his previous rudeness by showering Molly with effusive compliments, constantly refilling her cranberry juice until she felt bloated, trying to force vodka on her, generally being attentive and obnoxious. She would have hated it but for one interesting fact. All Willy's overbearing attentions seemed to have a most satisfying effect on Patrick, just as Toby's had the night before.

Her husband might not want her, but he sure as hell didn't want anyone else to touch her, even as elderly a lecher as Uncle Willy. He stared at them with a sour expression, and she knew he wanted to send her up to bed as he had the previous nights.

But she had no intention of behaving like a

naughty little girl. Her behavior was exemplary, annoying him even further, and it was well past eleven when she finally left them. She had learned a lot that day, and had a lot more to learn. She knew where her money came from, and she had a fairly good idea of why Patrick had married her. Not because of the money, but out of pity for the poor infatuated teenager. The notion was intensely painful.

She fell into bed feeling waterlogged and exhausted, and dreamed of Patrick, staring at her out of brooding eyes.

IT SHOULDN'T HAVE bothered him, Patrick thought. That lost expression in her eyes, when he'd thrown her infatuation back in her face. If she really couldn't remember it, why should it have embarrassed her?

But suddenly he remembered what it was like. He'd just come back home after two years away, his most recent exodus the result of his worst parental battle to date. He'd gone places, seen things, done things he still hated to think about, and he felt dirty, cruel and worthless. Until he'd looked down into the sixteen-year-old eyes of his father's latest stray and seen a shining adoration he'd never deserved.

He couldn't resist it, as much as he tried. She worshiped the ground he walked on, even taking his part in battles with his formidable father.

And instead of further inciting Jared Winters's wrath, she'd merely made his father retreat with a crafty smile.

She was pretty, she was smart, she was brave, and

she was unbearably loyal. If he'd been ten years younger. If she'd been someone other than his father's handpicked consort...

As it was, he'd ignored his zipper, treated her like the younger sister he'd never had, and kept his hands to himself. Each year it grew harder, and each year he was more determined to keep her at a distance. And each year his father's goading and Molly's innocent adoration eroded his determination.

He gave in, at last. After his father's sudden death from a heart attack, after the will was read and she was crying, desperate to make him take all that money that she'd never wanted. He'd come up with the obvious, logical answer, one that would salve her pride, support the expense of Winter's Edge farm, and please the ghost of his father.

Not to mention the fact that he wanted it, wanted her so badly that it was eating him alive.

He thought he'd gotten over that during their ten months of married life. She'd done her best to cure him, but he should have known better. All he had to do was look down into those innocent, green-blue eyes, and it all came rushing back.

But this time he wouldn't give in. He could keep the place going without the substantial amount his father had left her. A little economy, a lot of hard work, and things would be fine.

That was just what he needed. To work so hard he wouldn't have time to think. To remember. To want what he couldn't have.

To work so hard he'd be free of her. At last.

Chapter Seven

At six-thirty the next morning, Molly leaned over the side of her bed and threw up all over the fluffy white carpet. She rolled onto her back with bemused satisfaction. At least now something would have to be done about this awful room, she thought, and was sick again. She was too weak and dizzy to even try to make it to the bathroom, and she leaned back with a throbbing head against the immense pillows that adorned her bed.

There was no longer any way she could ignore the inevitable. She ate all the time, slept too much, and threw up every morning. Put that on top of a memory loss and the personal history of a slut, and there was only one logical explanation.

She was pregnant.

The notion both horrified and enchanted her. She looked down at her flat stomach and imagined it, round and full with a baby. She ran a tentative hand across it and found she could smile. It was a perfect image, but only with the right father to complete the picture.

It was only logical to assume that Patrick was the father. After all, he was her husband, albeit a not very enthusiastic one.

A baby might mend the brokenness between them. But she didn't want a baby for marriage therapy, she wanted Patrick's baby because she...well, she just wanted Patrick's baby.

But what if the baby was someone else's? The man she'd run away with? Or any of the scores of lovers she'd supposedly enjoyed?

She still wanted that baby. And nothing and no one would take it away from her.

She also wasn't going to exist in a state of limbo any longer, now that she'd faced the shocking probability. She wanted answers, she wanted proof. She wanted to buy baby clothes.

She climbed out of bed, slowly and carefully, but all traces of illness seemed to have passed except for a slight weakness in her knees. She moved to the window and flung it open, letting in the fresh cool air to cleanse the room.

The sun was shining for once, proving that Pennsylvania wasn't always covered with rain or dark, brooding clouds. There was the softest hint of spring in the air, a mere suggestion of warmth and growing things, but it was enough to give Molly one of her first feelings of optimism. She showered and dressed in record time, cleaned up the mess beside the bed, and prepared to deal with the hand fate had dealt her.

"Who's my doctor?" she asked as she walked into the kitchen. Mrs. Morse already had a cup of coffee ready for her, but she paused in the act of handing it to her, clearly startled.

"What's wrong? Are you having aftereffects from your accident? We can get in touch with the hospital in New Jersey…"

"No, I just need a regular doctor. Whoever I usually see." She took a tentative sip of the coffee, wondering how it would sit on her troubled stomach.

"You want to tell me why?"

Molly looked at her. Mrs. Morse was her only ally in this house full of angry strangers, and yet, for some reason she was loath to say anything. Perhaps she was afraid saying it aloud would make it go away. Maybe she was equally frightened that saying it aloud would make it more real.

"I just thought I needed a checkup," she said casually. "It's nothing to worry about, Mrs. Morse. I thought I ought to do something about birth control." True enough, in a way, she thought to herself.

"I'll give Dr. Turner a call for you," she offered.

"I'll take care of it myself. If you could just find me her number I'll call her when I get back from my walk. I need to get away from here for a little while, out in the fresh air."

Mrs. Morse paused, a startled expression on her face. "That's something," she said.

"What?"

"You knew Dr. Turner was a woman."

It never failed to unnerve her, these lightning flashes of knowledge that came without warning. "Maybe my memory's coming back," she said lightly.

"Maybe," Mrs. Morse said in a worried voice. "Let me just make you some bacon and eggs before you go out…"

"No, thanks!" Molly replied hastily, not feeling quite as recovered as she'd thought. The very idea of food was enough for her stomach to cramp up, and she set her coffee mug down, barely touched. "I'll have something later."

She rushed out into the early April sunshine, taking deep gulps of the clean wet air, and suddenly had the mad, determined desire to run. She took off at a comfortable lope, her body falling into the rhythm of it with effortless grace. She moved past the farm buildings, past the startled ducks, past Ben, her long hair streaming behind her, her heart pumping with a mindless joy.

She wanted to run forever, but she knew instinctively that she hadn't paced herself. After a bit she slowed, reluctantly, her heart pounding against her ribs, her breath rasping in her lungs. Her body wasn't as responsive as it had once been—she knew that without being sure how. She'd grown soft, her stamina had shattered. Perhaps it was the new life that might be growing inside her. She could only hope so.

The trees overhead were in bud, the winter brown-gray had a blush of green upon it, and all around her was the smell of wet spring earth. She inhaled it like a strong drug, wondering whether anyone could feel hopeless on a perfect day like this one, with the rich puffs of fleecy white clouds rolling around in the bluest of blue skies, and the soft spring breeze blowing in her face. As she continued down the narrow dirt track at a more moderate pace she was filled with a new hope, a new resolution that nothing could quite shake.

She hadn't gone less than a quarter of a mile when a sudden noise from the underbrush that lined the dirt road startled her into stopping. There was an eerie prickling at the back of her neck. Someone was watching her. Someone, or something, that wanted to hurt her.

She almost laughed out loud when she recognized Beastie's lumbering form charging down the road, knocking her flat on her back as he greeted her. She hugged him exuberantly, receiving a thorough face cleaning in return, then challenged him to a race down to the pile of rubble some ways in the distance.

He beat her, of course, and was waiting with ill-concealed canine smugness when she finally reached him, panting and gasping. And then she recognized where she was.

It was the charred remains of the barn she had supposedly burned down. Even after five long weeks the smell of wet, charred wood hung in the air. A part of one wall was standing, and she could imagine the flames crackling around the old structure, could even hear the screams of the poor tortured horses, could smell the sickening smell of burning flesh. She sank to the ground, dizzy, faint, and put her head between her knees.

"Are you all right?" She heard a soft voice nearby, and she looked up, blinking in the bright sunlight, to see Toby staring at her through the wire-rimmed glasses, his eyes dark and intense, his voice full of a soft concern that should have warmed her. She told herself it did, and yet she thought of Patrick.

She nodded, pulling herself together with a concerted effort and smiling up at him. "I just felt a little dizzy for a moment," she said. "I'd forgotten that I'm supposed to take it easy for a while." She looked at the incriminating ruins with sick eyes. "This…this must be the barn that burned."

He moved closer, sunlight glinting off the glasses and making his expression unreadable. "Don't you remember anything? Anything at all?"

"Not a thing," she said, resting her chin on her knees, trying to keep the guilt and misery out of her voice. Toby might have missed it, but Beastie was more attuned to her, and he whined softly, pushing his huge muzzle against her face.

Toby dropped down beside her, lying in the damp spring grass. "I've never heard of such a thing happening. Such a total absence of memory. Usually there are threads, pieces of the past."

"And what would you know about it?" She kept the edge out of her voice. "Are you a doctor?"

"No. I was in premed, until illness forced me to drop out. But I remember enough to know that this is a highly unlikely scenario."

"Whether amnesia happens this way or not, Toby, in my case it has," she said firmly. "I assume it will all come back eventually, but I'm not going to waste my time worrying about it. You shouldn't either.'' She smiled reassuringly. For some reason Toby seemed to bring out her maternal instincts, which was odd, since he appeared to be several years older than she was, perhaps more than that, if he was Patrick's contemporary. But added to those strong, maternal feelings was an obscure, cynical part of her that didn't quite trust his ingenuous charm—something about him didn't seem quite right. Something in the intensity of his gaze, in the faint edge to his voice.

Her imagination had to be working overtime, she thought in disgust. She didn't have enough memories to fill her brain, so she was making things up to keep herself busy. Toby Pentick was harmless. Sweet, friendly, and far nicer than her soon to be ex-husband. So why was she looking for trouble where none existed?

"And you're sure you really remember nothing?" Toby murmured with an intensity that seemed unnatural, and she stared at him in surprise.

"Nothing," she said smoothly. "Do you?"

He paled suddenly, and she realized she had struck a nerve. "What do you mean by that?"

"I mean do you remember anything about that night? Were you here? Did you see anything?"

He shook his head. "I was on the West Coast, visiting some friends. I had no idea anything had happened when I arrived back."

There was no missing the sorrow or concern in his voice. Her memory might be gone, but her instincts were still strong. Toby cared about her. Perhaps too much.

The next thought was sudden, inevitable, and devastating. Here was another man, a close friend. He might be the father of her child, and not her husband at all. "Toby?" she asked in an urgent voice. "Were we lovers?"

He blushed. It astonished her, the deep, red color mottling his skin as he stared at her. "No," he said stiffly. "Pat's my friend. I wouldn't do that to him."

Before she had the chance to probe further, he rose. "I'd better get back," he said in a strained voice. "I promised Pat I'd take a look at one of the mares. See you."

"All right," she said in a gentle voice, taking pity on his obvious mortification. She wouldn't have thought a grown man would be quite so sensitive. "I think I'll stay here for a while. Could you take Beastie back with you?" she asked. "He's a little overwhelming for a playmate—I don't think I'm quite up to managing him yet."

"Sure." He relaxed slightly. "Uh...don't stay out here alone too long, okay?"

She caught the faintest trace of worry in his voice, and she stared at him sharply. "Why not?"

He shook his head. "I just have the feeling that it's not particularly safe around here."

Molly stiffened her back, trying to ignore the chill of foreboding she felt at his words. "For me or for everyone?"

"For you," he said, and calling Beastie, he started down the road.

She rose up on her knees, determined to call after him, demand an explanation, but he was moving so fast there was no way she could catch him, short of sprinting, and she'd used up her energy for the morning. And she wasn't quite sure if Toby would answer her questions no matter how persistent she was.

Molly sank back in the damp brown grass and shut her eyes, trying to shut out the words of warning and bring back the feelings of peace and hope of a short while ago. But Toby's warning had done its job, and she sat up and looked around her nervously, wishing she hadn't banished Beastie. There were too many scorched and blackened trees around the ruins of the old barn, too much dark underbrush that could shield too many dangerous creatures. Dangerous creatures like Patrick, she wondered? She rose and moved closer to the barn, drawn to the blackened foundations and charred timbers, staring down at them. She had the eerie feeling that there were eyes on her, and she whirled suddenly, staring determinedly into the surrounding woods.

Of course there was no one there. She felt like an idiot as she turned back and leaned over the precipice of the barn, trying to peer into the old stone cellar of the building. She thought she saw something bright down there, something metal and flashing. Moving closer still, she suddenly felt herself hurtling face forward into the fire-blackened pit.

She must have bounced off one of the fallen beams, for she felt a sharp pain in her side, and something tore at her arm as she plummeted downward into the murky cellar. She hit bottom after what seemed like an endless fall, and she lay there in the mud, her body aching from the various obstructions she had hit on her way down, the feel of someone's hands as they pushed her still strong on her back. Without moving she could see her arm, see the long, narrow gash that was welling with dark blood. Blood that was rapidly pooling beneath her.

Her first thought was for the child that might or might not exist. Her entire body ached, but there was no worrisome cramping. The cut in her arm seemed by far the worst of her injuries, and she viewed it with sick fascination.

I'm going to bleed to death, she thought numbly. *It won't matter whether I'm pregnant or not—I'll be dead and no one will find me for years and years, and in the meantime Patrick will have all my money to spend on that woman.*

She squeezed her eyes shut, allowing her a few brief moments of misery and panic. And then she shot them open again. Life would be far too convenient if she just disappeared. She wasn't going to give them what they wanted again.

She rolled onto her back, groaning. The sides of the old cellar were oozing springtime mud, the sun filtered through the remaining beams above her and the gash in her arm no longer seemed quite so desperate. She still felt sick and weak, but from somewhere in the back of her brain came the memory that blood usually had that effect on her. Especially her own.

And then she heard the sound again, the low whine. "Beastie," she croaked weakly, but the sound was barely audible. "Beastie," she tried again, but it was useless.

There was a great crashing of wood, and an old beam thundered down, missing her head by inches. "What the hell are you doing down there?" Patrick's angry voice demanded. Molly had never heard anything so annoyingly welcome in her entire life.

"Taking a nap," she snapped. "What did you think?"

But he was gone again, and she almost called after him. He couldn't have left her there, could he? But then, what did she really know about him? Maybe he wanted to finish what he started.

And then she heard a crashing about at the far end of the structure, and she closed her eyes in relief. He hadn't left her. If he'd been the one to push her he would hardly have come to rescue her. In a moment he was beside her, his eyes dark with a fear and an anger that were both oddly comforting. "Are you all right?" he asked unnecessarily, poking at her arm.

"I...I guess so," she stammered weakly. "I hurt my arm, but that's about it. I think."

"You did, indeed," he said grimly, his hands gentle as he probed for possible damage. She didn't like it, the impersonal feel of his hands on her body, touching her with the same care and interest he might show a wounded horse. Perhaps less. "And it serves you right," he added. "What the hell do you mean, wandering around here? It's dangerous; any fool would know that! Did you have some incredible urge to return to the scene of the crime, to see how much damage you did? If it weren't for Beastie I might never have found you.''

During this tirade he managed to lift her up in his arms with a tenderness at amazing variance with the harshness in his voice, and he carried her out into the brilliant sunlight by the remaining flight of stone steps.

"Are you always so angry?" she asked wearily, leaning her head against his shoulder, too weak and tired to fight.

"With you, yes," he answered grimly, stalking down the road and jarring her poor, bruised body with every step.

"How did you happen to fall? Didn't you have enough sense to keep your distance from the edge? Or were you too fascinated by the ruins...?"

"I didn't fall. I was pushed."

The silence that followed was overwhelming, and she half expected him to drop her in the middle of the road. He didn't, but his expression grew even more grim.

"Still dramatizing, Molly?" he drawled in an unpleasant voice. "I would have thought you'd get tired of being the center of attention all the time."

"You don't believe me?" she demanded, fury wiping out the last of her shock and fear.

"Not for a moment. No one else would either, so you might as well save your breath. Why would anyone want to shove you down in the cellar? If they were trying to kill you there are a lot more effective ways."

She shoved at him, desperate to break his hold on her, but she'd forgotten how strong he was. He simply tightened his grip, almost painfully, as he stalked toward the house, and she gave up her fruitless struggle as a belated, comforting thought hit her. His anger at her story, his disbelief, was honest. If he refused to believe she'd been pushed, then he couldn't be the one who'd pushed her. The true culprit would have lied to cover for himself, or tried to throw suspicion on someone else. Her enemy, her nemesis, had to be someone else.

She was almost smiling by the time they reached the house. She sat in the kitchen, watching her husband glower at her, while Mrs. Morse clucked and moaned in distress and Uncle Willy, who was already slightly the worse for alcohol at such an early hour, kept his pale, watery eyes averted from the steadily oozing blood as he tried to make encouraging noises.

Dr. Turner arrived, a grumpy, middle-age woman who seemed annoyed at being bothered. She poked at Molly, with even less care than Patrick had evinced, bandaged her up, and pronounced her none the worse for a little shock, all with an audience of interested bystanders. "But you should be more careful, Mrs. Winters," she said gravely, snapping her battered case shut. "All you'll feel is a little stiffness. It could have been a lot worse. You could have hit your head again, and then we'd have to put you in the hospital for observation. I imagine you've had enough of hospitals for the time being."

"Yes, Dr. Turner," she murmured in a docile

voice, thoughts racing through her head. She could have been killed. And someone *had* pushed her, she knew it as well as she... Well, she didn't know anything about herself too well, but she knew that she'd been pushed. Patrick had already made it clear that no one would believe her, and she didn't bother trying to explain. If no one would listen, why should she waste her breath?

Except that Patrick was watching her with an odd expression behind the annoyance in those blue, blue eyes. Maybe he believed her after all. Maybe he knew she'd been pushed because he was the one who'd pushed her, and he'd been afraid to finish her off for fear Toby would return and see him.

Dr. Turner was already heading for the door. Molly racked her brain, trying to think of a discreet way to call her back. Finally, Mrs. Morse spoke up.

"Wasn't there something you wanted to ask Dr. Turner about, Molly?"

Four pairs of eyes turned to stare at her, with Patrick's being the most suspicious.

"Well, young lady?" Dr. Turner demanded when Molly didn't say anything. "Is this an emergency?"

"Er...no."

"Then call my office and make an appointment like everyone else. I've already been here too long as it is. Next time, Patrick, you take her to the emergency room."

"There isn't going to be a next time," Patrick said in a quiet voice. And Molly wasn't sure whether to be pleased or terrified.

"I think you'd better spend the rest of the day in

bed," Patrick announced after Dr. Turner had left. "And from now on you aren't allowed out unless someone goes with you."

"But why?" she demanded, then winced in pain. She lowered her voice. "This was just an accident—it won't happen again."

"You go out with someone or you don't go out at all," he said in the kind of voice that brooked no arguments. "And if you disobey me I'll lock you in."

"Disobey you?" she echoed in a tight little voice. "Who the hell do you think you are, my father? You can't tell me what to do."

"I doubt even your father told you what to do," he said sourly, and without another word he stormed out of the house, leaving Molly in a state of stomach-churning rage.

"Well," said Mrs. Morse after a moment, "who would have thought he'd get so worked up?" She shook her head, but there was an oddly hopeful expression in her eyes. "Don't you worry, Molly. I'll fix you some nice hot soup and ham sandwiches, and some of my chocolate cake. How would you like that?"

She was hungry again. If she had been pregnant in the morning, she obviously still was. "I'd love it. Will you join me, Uncle Willy?" she asked politely of the silent figure in the corner.

He shook his head in faint disgust, the neat orange strands carefully combed over that pink and shining skull. "No, thank you, my dear. I always partake of only the lightest meal when I first wake up." He rose and wandered out of the kitchen, looking oddly disturbed about something. He hardly seemed sensitive enough to be worried about her well-being, and Molly watched his retreating figure with vague, shapeless suspicions.

"All right, Molly," Mrs. Morse said, coming to stand in front of her with arms planted on her ample hips. "What's going on?"

"What do you mean? I must have tripped..."

"I'm not talking about your fall. Assuming it really was a fall, though it seems to me Patrick's right about your being more careful. No, I want to know why you wanted to see Dr. Turner in private. And don't tell me some story about you needing birth control, because I don't believe it."

She looked up at her. When it came right down to it, she had to trust someone. "I think I'm pregnant."

"Sweet heavens!" Mrs. Morse said. "Have you told Patrick yet?"

"Not until I'm certain. What if it's not his?"

Mrs. Morse's face fell. "I hadn't thought of that. You couldn't be very far along—they would have caught it in the hospital after your accident."

"And since I haven't been home in five weeks that would mean that Patrick..."

"Wasn't the father," Mrs. Morse finished for her. "Why don't you ask him?"

"Not until I have to. Not until I see Dr. Turner and get the proof. She should know how far along I am."

"Molly, dearest," she said in a gentler voice,

"there's no need to be scared of Pat. I don't know what's gone on between the two of you, but for all his bluster he's a caring, decent man."

"Sure," Molly said with just a trace of bitterness. "He cares about Lisa Canning."

"He cares about you, missy."

Molly shook her head, unwilling to accept the notion. "You're not to say anything until I find out. In the meantime I suppose I need to get an appointment."

"I'll call for you," Mrs. Morse said firmly. "No one needs to know anything about it—we'll just tell anyone who asks that you were feeling dizzy after your fall."

"You don't suppose that I...did anything to it?"

She shook her head, an ancient sorrow shadowing the eyes behind the steel-rimmed glasses. "You'd feel it if you did bring on a miscarriage, believe me. I had six of them myself, before the doctor told me to stop trying, and there's no ignoring the symptoms, no matter how early along you are. No, if you're pregnant then nothing's happened to it yet." She rose. "Should I call her office?"

Molly nodded numbly.

She was lost in thought when Mrs. Morse returned a few minutes later. "Damned receptionist. You'd think Dr. Turner was the Queen of England and not some small-town family practitioner. She can't see you till the day after tomorrow, unless it's an emergency. In the meantime the best thing for you to do is go upstairs and lie down and try not to

think about it. Find yourself a good book or something."

"I've read them all," she said morosely, rising
slowly from the hard chair. "Maybe I'll explore the
house."

"Whatever for?"

"Because I don't remember it," she said simply.
"And I'm not at all tired."

"Well, you be careful if you go in the attics.
There's a lot of junk stored up there," she warned.
"I'd come with you but your Aunt Ermy is coming
in on the 5:47 train tonight and the Lord knows I'd
better have an elegant enough supper to suit her pal-
ate. You go on ahead and come down here for some
brownies and tea later on if you feel like it."

"I will," she promised, setting off.

ANOTHER MISTAKE. Another botched attempt. All
she'd ended up with was a gashed arm. Things were
not going according to plan, not in the slightest, and
it was getting more than frustrating.

Sooner or later someone was going to start getting
suspicious at all her mishaps. It wouldn't matter if
Molly suspected something—her credibility was in
the toilet already. No one would listen to her.

The local police didn't give a damn. Stroup
wanted to get into her pants and nothing more, and
Ryker was so far off base there was nothing to worry
about. Not yet.

But there couldn't be any more mistakes. Sooner
or later it was going to come back to her. She didn't
remember—there was no longer any doubt of that.

Her green-blue eyes were totally guileless; she hadn't the faintest idea whom she could trust.

But that happy state of affairs wouldn't last forever. Next time they were going to do it right. Get it right.

Get her dead. And silent.

Chapter Eight

Molly couldn't rid herself of the feeling that she was Alice in Wonderland, or Dorothy in Oz. The house had grown increasingly familiar over the last two days—the beautifully comfortable living room, the formal dining room, the kitchen, the neat and uninspiring little office under the stairs where Patrick did his accounts and hid from his wife.

But upstairs was a different matter. Patrick's closed door was an enticing Pandora's box, but even Molly's courage had limits. She could explore it later, when she was sure he was nowhere around. Perhaps even tonight, while he was out picking up the mysterious Aunt Ermy from the train station.

She needed to see if she could find something to jog her memory. A hint, a clue, some tiny something to jar her stubborn mind. The longer it remained blank the more frustrated she grew.

She wasn't sure she really was in any kind of danger. Even though she'd been involved in a murder, no one had seemed interested in harming her now. So far, no one had seemed particularly interested in getting within touching distance of her.

But Patrick had touched. Unwillingly, almost as if he couldn't help himself. And she knew he wanted to touch her again. Almost as much as she wanted him to touch her.

Aunt Ermy's room was a jumble of clutter. Little ornaments jostled each other for space on her mantelpiece, her cherry wood dressers, her Queen Anne secretary. Every spare inch in the room was filled with an artifact of some sort, from exquisite pieces to the merely shoddy. Dresden ballerinas danced with plastic penguins, there were plump, overstuffed pillows everywhere, and the room felt claustrophobic. She shut the door behind her, unable to rid herself of the notion that she didn't have very much in common with Aunt Ermy.

Uncle Willy's room was exactly the opposite— practically devoid of personal clutter. That was an empty vodka bottle in his wastepaper basket, and the clothes he wore yesterday were neatly folded and placed on a Windsor chair. The atmosphere of the room was stale and tired, rather like Uncle Willy himself, and she left just as quickly.

The attics lay beyond the little turn in the hallway, down two steps and past the linen closet and the guest bathroom. She turned the doorknob, not without a small shiver of apprehension. Since this morning she distrusted being alone. It seemed to her as if there were eyes everywhere, watching her, threatening her.

"This is ridiculous," she muttered out loud, stepping into the room and switching on the light.

Mrs. Morse hadn't exaggerated when she said the attics were filled with junk. Trunks upon trunks upon trunks, ancient newspapers and magazines tied in neat little bundles, old pieces of riding tack, skis, tennis rackets needing restringing, boxes and boxes and boxes. And her furniture.

She recognized it with a swift feeling of relief and love, rather like seeing an old friend, and she moved toward it in a daze, running her hand over the warm glow of the cherry bedstead, the delicate dressing table, the blanket chest that somehow seemed to fit with the various periods of the other pieces. She was going to have it back, she promised herself. As soon as she could have that hideous modern stuff removed and carted off to the dump, she'd have her own beloved pieces back in there.

She went over to the most readily available boxes, hoping that something else might jog her memory. But nothing else tripped that frustrating, mysterious little mechanism in her brain. The prom dress that hung forlornly must have been hers, yet she remembered no magic, breathless moments, no starry-eyed excitement connected with it. It was simply a pretty dress, worn by a girl she didn't know, and she wondered vaguely where her wedding dress was. And whether it would bring her any greater recognition.

She lost track of time, poking and prying and trying to force some shred of memory. Hours might have passed. She made a mental note of all the furniture she knew belonged in her room, and lost herself in schemes on how best to arrange it. When she finally left the room and switched the light off behind her, the hallway was dark. She could hear a car driving away from the house, and she hurried to look out her bedroom window.

It was the fairly new Mercedes that she knew belonged to Patrick, and she breathed a sigh of relief. She would have time now to snoop through his room. There was no other word for it—she needed to discover the secrets he kept from his unwanted wife. Any clue to the impasse they were currently in was worth prying for, even if her methods were less than honorable. She had to find out more about him if she was ever going to remember all she had lost. And why she had married him in the first place.

And whether she had any reason to fear him.

She still wasn't quite sure why she was afraid of him. He certainly didn't seem the sort of man to be abusive. There was anger, deep inside him, and a lot of that anger was directed at her. But she still couldn't believe he'd deliberately want to injure her.

Or could she believe it? Was she a fool to trust her instincts when she had no memory to back them up? Why couldn't Patrick have bashed old Ben on the head and set the barn fire? Insurance money could be a very strong motive.

Maybe he'd paid George Andrews to lure her away and kill her. Maybe he'd tried to kill her himself.

Maybe, maybe, maybe. There were times when she thought she'd go crazy if she didn't start to find some answers to the questions that plagued her.

Including the most basic. Was her husband a dangerous enemy or a disinterested bystander? Or someone who cared more than he wanted to?

She pulled the thick cotton sweater she'd bought him out of her drawer and tucked it under her arm before attempting her final excursion. If she happened to run into Mrs. Morse or Uncle Willy at least she would have an excuse. Though why she should need an excuse to enter her husband's bedroom was beyond her comprehension. She simply knew it to be the truth.

She moved silently down the hall and opened Patrick's door with all the stealth of a master criminal. Not a sound emanated from the upstairs hall. For all anyone would know she was sound asleep in the elegant nightmare called her room. She slipped inside and shut the door.

She hadn't looked very carefully when she had explored the first day, simply noticing the air of unfrilly masculinity before she'd shut the door again. But now it had taken on an entirely new dimension. It belonged to Patrick, the enigma, and as such was endlessly fascinating.

His bed was high and wide, at least three and a half feet off the floor, the kind of bed where babies are born and old people die. The kind of bed to found a dynasty in, if one was so inclined. She ran a hand over the beautiful quilt, and wondered whether she had shared any unforgettable moments in this enticing bed. If so, she had obviously forgotten them.

She could imagine Patrick's long, lean body, tossing and turning in so large a bed, and she felt a queer little twinge in her stomach. Of longing? Or nervousness? Or both? She couldn't truthfully answer.

She placed the sweater on the bed with great care, then moved to the dresser, noting the silver-backed combs with his initials engraved on them, the loose change lying around. The photograph of a young girl standing in a field, her head thrown back, laughing from sheer joy.

Molly's hand was trembling as she reached out and took the picture. She knew that face, that moment. It was a picture of her, not that old, and she could almost remember, almost grasp...

"What the hell are you doing in here?" His voice was rough, shocking, sending whatever she was about to remember flying into a million pieces. She stared at him numbly.

He shut the door behind him and moved closer. He'd unbuttoned his shirt and pulled it free from his jeans, obviously on the way to a shower, and it was all she could do to keep her eyes away from his chest.

She had to have seen men's chests before. She had to have seen this particular one before, and she was being an utter fool to stand there, speechless. So he was tanned, even at the end of winter. So he was lean, and strong, with a triangle of hair that arrowed down toward his jeans. So it was a very nice chest indeed. There was still no need for her to suddenly find herself unable to breathe.

He moved closer, and there was just the hint of a threat in his movements, and a sinuous grace that made her look around helplessly for means to escape.

"What are you doing with a picture of me on your dresser?" she countered, trying to divert him from whatever he had in mind.

"It's not you," he said flatly. "It's a girl I once knew, but she's been gone for years. Leaving you in her place." His voice was contemptuous as he surveyed her, and then he shrugged, never slowing his determined progress toward her as she stood guiltily in the corner of his bedroom. "Call it an old weakness," he added slowly. He stopped, directly in front of her, so close she could feel his body heat, so close she could see the tiny fan of lines around his stormy blue eyes.

Her reaction made no sense to her. She wanted to run away, and she wanted to touch him. She wanted to reach out and run her hand down that lean, muscled chest, but something, some innate wisdom, stopped her. Despite the fact that she must have done that, and much more, in the past, she knew she shouldn't do it now. No matter how much she wanted to feel the warmth of his skin beneath her hand.

"You know, Molly," he said in a low, sinuous voice, "you should have told me you wanted to visit my bedroom. I would have invited you long ago."

Quite casually he reached out and took her by the shoulders, drawing her unresisting body towards him. "It's amazing that you still have some effect on me." His voice was rough, and his mouth covered hers with a sudden force that left her shocked, stunned, paralyzed. He held her in an unbreakable grip as he caught her chin in his hand and continued to kiss her, with slow, contemptuous deliberation, refusing to allow her to escape, until she was a shaking, trembling mass of confused reactions, reactions she was powerless to control. And then his mouth softened, and it was no longer punishment but a reward, and she kissed him back, sliding her arms around his waist, pressing up against him with helpless longing she hadn't quite understood.

She needed to be here. Locked tight against him, his mouth on hers, demanding nothing but complete surrender. She made a quiet little sound in the back of her throat, and surrender it was.

He pulled away, suddenly, moving back from her as if she'd suddenly become contagious. "Damn you," he said in a low, furious voice. "Get out of here."

She stared at him through the twilight room for a moment, shaken, shocked to the very core of her being. And then she ran from the room without a backward glance. Ran from him as she had run before, five weeks earlier, in the same blind panic.

When she reached her room she slammed the door shut behind her and locked it with a loud, satisfying click. Leaning against the door, she trembled in the aftermath of his touch. She had surely never been kissed like that before. She couldn't have forgotten such a torrent of emotions. As a matter of fact, she could have sworn that she'd never been kissed at all—the feel of a hot, wet mouth against hers had been a startling revelation.

But that was absurd. She was twenty-three years old, and married. Her mind must be playing even more sadistic tricks on her.

She moved through her darkened room and threw herself onto the bed. She wouldn't go down to dinner, she promised herself. She couldn't face him after...that...that.

She would lie there and starve.

"MOLLY? Molly, dear, open up. Open up right now!" An imperative voice broke through Molly's sleep-numbed mind, and she sat up dazedly. It took her a moment to remember where she was, and what had happened. Patrick's mouth on hers, the too-brief moment that had burned into her brain.

Unfortunately nothing else had disrupted her blank memory. She probed, looking for answers, ignoring the incessant pounding at her door. Still nothing.

"Who is it?" she finally called out groggily, switching on the light.

"Your Aunt Ermintrude, of course. Now open the door immediately."

What a tyrant, she thought. "What can I do for you?" she called out with deliberate calm.

"What do you mean, what can you do for me? Do as I say immediately, Molly, or I shan't answer for the consequences." Her deep contralto voice rose to a tiny squeak of rage.

"Then don't," Molly answered mildly enough, glad to have an instinct confirmed. She couldn't stand dear Aunt Ermy. "I'll open the door when I'm ready to, and not before. Go away and leave me alone.''

There was an outraged silence beyond the oak door, and she could picture a rather Wagnerian lady bristling with indignation. After a moment or two she heard angry, stomping footsteps walk away and she chuckled, inordinately pleased that she had managed to rout some member of her hostile family at last.

"Molly." Mrs. Morse's soft voice broke through her pleased reverie, and she sprang up. The woman darted into the room as soon as Molly unlocked it, with a furtive glance over her shoulder to make sure she was unobserved.

"My, my, you have put your aunt in a taking," she said with satisfaction. "Sent me up here to find out what in hell was going on with you."

Molly threw herself back down on the bed, wondering absently whether she looked any different. Could Mrs. Morse see that Patrick had kissed her? Probably not—people were kissed all the time. Everyone had made it clear she'd done a lot more than kissing, and with a number of men besides her husband. It was hardly the soul-shattering event it seemed to her overwrought imagination. "I don't care much for Aunt Ermy," Molly said in a meditative voice.

"Well, now that's a new thing, I must say. You and the old battle-ax used to be inseparable buddies, always tearing poor Patrick apart each chance you got." She sniffed. "I'm glad you've seen the error of your ways."

"We don't seem to have much in common," Molly said. "Are you sure?"

"I'm sure," she said flatly. "I'm just glad that's over and done with. I came to find out if you'd be coming down to dinner. There'll only be the three of you—Willy, Ermy, and you. Patrick took off about an hour ago in a towering rage. Said he wouldn't be in for dinner. I wondered if you would know anything about that?" Her curiosity was unabashed, but Molly wasn't in the mood to satisfy it.

"Can't imagine." She scrambled off the bed. "And of course I'll be down to dinner. Can I give you a hand?"

"It's all done. Everything to her highness's liking, you can be sure." She pursed her thin lips in disgust. "You can come down and keep her off my back, though. She and Willy are having a high old time in the living room, drinking Patrick's liquor and heaping insults on him in his absence."

"I'll see what I can do," Molly promised, running a brush thought her hair and following Mrs. Morse's upright figure through the halls.

She paused at the entrance of the living room, just long enough to take stock of its inhabitants. Aunt Ermy was Wagnerian, all right, with a high-swept pompadour of silver hair and three determined chins, each one more determined than the last. Tiny, piglike eyes, a retroussé snout with a fierce mustache bristling beneath completed the picture, and of her massive body the less said the better: a mountainous bulk on tiny trotters. She looked as unpleasant as

Molly had imagined her to be, and she was mortally glad the relationship was, at best, a distant one.

"Good evening, everyone," she greeted them airily as she sailed into the room. Aunt Ermy's tiny eyes took in the jeans, the T-shirt, the lack of makeup, and her face screwed up into a look of pouting disapproval.

"Well," she said at length, "I'm pleased to see you finally decided to come down and greet your poor aunt after your long and mysterious absence. Going off like that without a word!"

Molly smiled at her, not a bit disturbed. "Sorry," she said briefly, helping herself to a large glass of cranberry juice and slipping into the hard-backed chair left—the two relatives having commandeered the most comfortable ones in the room. "Did you enjoy your visit?"

"I might well ask the same of you," Aunt Ermy said frostily. Molly eyed her with cold-blooded calm, and she immediately changed her domineering attitude. "Molly, dear, couldn't you have told us where you were going? We were *worried* about you!"

Molly shrugged, and Aunt Ermy leaned closer, the air heavy with the expensive but unsuitably girlish scent she had splashed all over her. "And Willy here tells me you've lost your memory. Surely you can't have forgotten your Aunt Ermy? And all the fun things we used to do together?"

"I'm afraid I have," she said in a brisk voice. "I'm starving. Mrs. Morse should have dinner ready by now—shall we go in?" Molly rose gracefully, and Aunt Ermy stared up at her with increasing annoyance.

"Well, really, Molly, we've hardly started on our second drink," she began, but Molly interrupted her.

"Oh, that's perfectly all right, you can bring it in with you," she said, nipping her protests in the bud. Uncle Willy looked up from his chair, a gleam of amusement and something else fighting through the sodden expression on his face. He wandered after them into the dining room, bringing not only his glass but the crystal decanter of whiskey with him.

Molly watched Aunt Ermy bear down on the seat at the head of the table like a steamship. As soon as she pulled out the heavy chair Molly darted into the seat, smiling at her with all the charm she had at her beck and call. "Thank you, Aunt Ermy," she said sweetly, pulling out the heavy linen napkin and placing it on her lap.

Ermintrude stood there for a moment in a floundering rage, immovable and furious. She seated herself with awful majesty at Molly's right, her mountainous form quivering with indignation.

"You used to dress for dinner, my dear," was all she said in an aggrieved tone, and Molly considered she'd gotten off lightly.

"I prefer to be comfortable, Aunt Ermy," she replied calmly.

"And where has *he* gone tonight?" she questioned halfway through the meal.

"Do you mean my husband?" Molly asked her politely. Whatever her differences were with the man, she wasn't about to let this awful old woman insult him. "He had some business to attend to, I believe."

"Business like *la belle dame* Canning, if I'm not mistaken," Willy snorted from the foot of the table.

"Perhaps," Molly said, undisturbed. "But I don't think that's any of your concern." Her calm statement put a damper on the dinner conversation, but by the time they were back in the living room and well fortified with additional alcohol Uncle Willy and Aunt Ermy grew quite loquacious once more.

"I'm glad to see you're drinking your cranberry juice," Aunt Ermy observed heavily as she accepted another tall glass from Willy's drink-fumbled hands. "At least you're following my precepts in that matter."

Molly immediately tried to refuse the drink, but Willy took no notice, trying to add a shot of vodka to the glass she held firmly out of reach.

"Come on, my girl," he pouted. "Don't go all prudish on us. You used to put away quite a bit of this stuff before your transformation into Rebecca of Sunnybrook Farm. Patrick's not here to see you— live a bit," he bantered clumsily.

Molly shook her head, frowning in annoyance. "This doesn't have anything to do with Patrick," she snapped irritably, remembering the feel of his hot mouth on hers. She shivered and sipped at the cranberry juice. She didn't want to drink. She didn't like the idea of alcohol, and if she really was pregnant it gave her an even stronger reason to abstain.

She wondered how her two so-called relatives would react to the notion of a pregnancy. With screams of horror, no doubt. She imagined Aunt Ermy would try to drag her off to the nearest abortion clinic if she could.

"Of course it doesn't have anything to do with Pat," Aunt Ermy chimed in. "Do you suppose my poor little girl would let herself be browbeaten by that towering bully? I warned him when I saw him tonight—I wouldn't stand by and let him order you about."

"And what did he say to that?" Molly asked curiously.

Uncle Willy snorted. "Told her what she could do with her advice, and that he'd order you about as much as he pleased. Ermy didn't care for that much, did you, dearie?" He laughed again, and the sound was a high-pitched giggle.

Molly rose suddenly, disgusted by the two of them. "I think I'll go up to bed," she said. "It's been a long day and I still don't feel recovered from this morning."

"Oh, yes, Willy was telling me about your accident." Was there a slight emphasis on the word accident? Aunt Ermy seemed all solicitude. "You really should be very careful, Molly dear. Certain people could find your death very convenient. Very convenient indeed. If I were you I wouldn't go out alone." She nodded her head meaningfully, and Molly calmly considered hitting her.

"Thank you for your concern, Aunt Ermy," she said in a deceptively even voice. "Patrick has already suggested the same thing. I'll be sure to take very good care of myself." She started out of the

room, Beastie at her side. He obviously cared no
more for those two than she herself did, Molly
thought gratefully.

"Don't forget your cranberry juice, Molly."
Willy placed the cool glass in her hand.

She took it with her, managing a tight-lipped
smile of thanks.

WELCOME TO THE
CASINO:
Try your luck at the Roulette Wheel ...
Play a hand of Twenty-One!

How to play:

1. Play the Roulette and Twenty-One scratch-off games, as instructed on the opposite page, to see that you are eligible for FREE BOOKS and a FREE GIFT!

2. Send back the card and you'll receive TWO brand-new Harlequin Intrigue® novels. These books have a cover price of $3.99 each in the U.S. and $4.50 each in Canada, but they are yours to keep absolutely free.

3. There's no catch. You're under no obligation to buy anything. We charge nothing — ZERO — for your first shipment. And you don't have to make any minimum number of purchases — not even one!

4. The fact is, thousands of readers enjoy receiving books by mail from the Harlequin Reader Service® before they're available in stores. They like the convenience of home delivery, and they love our discount prices!

5. We hope that after receiving your free books you'll want to remain a subscriber. But the choice is yours — to continue or cancel, any time at all!

So why not take us up on our invitation, with no risk of any kind. You'll be glad you did!

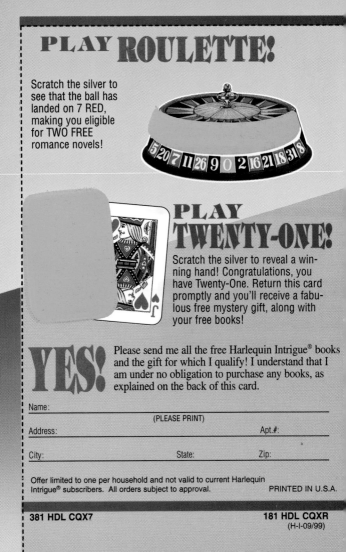

The Harlequin Reader Service® — Here's how it works:

Accepting your 2 free books and mystery gift places you under no obligation to buy anything. You may keep the books and gift and return the shipping statement marked "cancel." If you do not cancel, about a month later we'll send you 4 additional novels and bill you just $3.34 each in the U.S., or $3.71 each in Canada, plus 25¢ delivery per book and applicable taxes if any.* That's the complete price and — compared to the cover price of $3.99 in the U.S. and $4.50 in Canada — it's quite a bargain! You may cancel at any time, but if you choose to continue, every month we'll send you 4 more books, which you may either purchase at the discount price or return to us and cancel your subscription.

*Terms and prices subject to change without notice. Sales tax applicable in N.Y. Canadian residents will be charged applicable provincial taxes and GST.

If offer card is missing write to: Harlequin Reader Service, 3010 Walden Ave., P.O. Box 1867, Buffalo, NY 14240-9952

BUSINESS REPLY MAIL
FIRST-CLASS MAIL   PERMIT NO 717   BUFFALO NY

POSTAGE WILL BE PAID BY ADDRESSEE

HARLEQUIN READER SERVICE
3010 WALDEN AVE
PO BOX 1867
BUFFALO NY 14240-9952

NO POSTAGE
NECESSARY
IF MAILED
IN THE
UNITED STATES

Chapter Nine

He shouldn't have kissed her. He'd done a lot of stupid things in his life, so many he'd lost count, but kissing her yesterday had to be one of the worst.

He could make all sorts of excuses. She was standing in his darkened bedroom, looking up at him as if he were a cross between Jack the Ripper and Tom Cruise, acting as if she'd never seen a man's naked chest before. When he knew she'd seen a lot more.

He wasn't sure what made him put his hands on her. His mouth on hers. The anger that consumed him whenever he saw her, thought of her. Curiosity, to see just what she'd learned from all the men she'd been with.

He'd been tempting fate as well. Checking to see whether he could remain immune to her. He should have known he couldn't. The touch, the taste of her, had burned itself into his brain.

Why couldn't life be simple? Why couldn't he have fallen in love with someone like Lisa Canning? Lisa, who'd offer him everything and expect not much more than energetic sex and a certain tolerant discretion.

Why did he have to want someone like Molly?

It had been a mistake, but not a fatal one. So he'd kissed her. So he'd felt her arms, tight around him, and the tremor that rippled through her body. He'd heard that soft, plaintive sound she'd made in the back of her throat, and he'd frozen. He'd had the sense to push her away, send her away.

And he had the sense to keep away himself.

It wouldn't happen again. If worse came to worst he'd take what Lisa Canning had been offering so blatantly, just to get it out of his system.

Sooner or later Molly would grow tired of this charade, tell the police what they needed to know, and then he could get rid of her. And in doing so, he'd spike his father's final, biggest wish.

It had to be a charade. There was no way she could possibly be the wide-eyed innocent she appeared to be.

And it was his own stupid fault for wanting to believe her. Thinking with his hormones instead of his head.

She'd have to admit the truth. Whatever the hell the truth might be. And then the two of them could go their separate ways. Forever.

So why didn't the prospect seem more like a victory, instead of petty revenge?

SHE WAS SICK AGAIN the next morning. This time she didn't wreck the carpet—she had thoughtfully provided herself with an empty wastebasket on the chance that this morning would parallel the others. She was vaguely hoping against hope that she'd be well this morning: no little babies to complicate her life. But fate didn't want to cooperate. She lay back in bed, shivering with the aftermath.

This time she didn't fall back asleep. It was stormy again, and the steady beat of the rain seemed to pound even louder in her throbbing head. There was no point in delaying—she climbed wearily out of her oversoft bed and prepared to face the day.

There was no one stirring in the darkened kitchen. And no wonder—5:30 was a bit early even for a farm. She made a full pot of coffee, lit the fire that had already been laid in the hearth, and huddled close to it. Eventually, somewhere in the middle of her second cup of coffee, the rain slackened off a bit, and she listened to the noise of an approaching car with interest. It was her dear husband in the old van, presumably back from a night in the arms of the grieving widow. The surge of anger and jealousy that swept through Molly frightened her, and she put down the cup with trembling fingers.

She saw him long before he saw her. There was a cold, discontented look on his lean face, which pleased her enormously. It certainly wasn't the proper expression for a man returning from a satisfying night of love.

He ran in the door, shaking off the clinging raindrops from his long black hair. Then his eyes met hers, and he stopped dead.

"Good morning," she greeted him evenly, willing herself sternly to forget the last moment she had seen him, the overwhelming reaction she'd had to his kiss.

He moved closer into the room, relaxing slightly. "You're up early," he observed. "Is there any more coffee?"

"In the carafe." She picked up her cup and took another sip, the trembling in her hand down to a bare minimum. "How's Lisa?" She could have kicked herself for saying that.

"Fine," he said brusquely. "She sends you her love." And, taking his cup with him, he left the room.

Cursing herself for a fool, Molly rose from her seat and began puttering around the kitchen. She discovered a cache of day-old muffins and proceeded to heat them in the oven. Placing them daintily on one of the old Spode plates and adding butter and homemade jam, she carried them into Patrick's office.

He looked up from the paper he was staring at, and frowned. "A peace offering," she stated, before he could open his mouth to order her from the room. "I'm sorry for what I said in the kitchen. It was uncalled for." She didn't honestly believe that, but she expected Patrick wouldn't agree. "Would you like some more coffee?"

"I'll get it," he said, but she took the cup from him in a peremptory fashion.

"You eat your muffins," she said grandly, sailing from the room. In a moment she was back, with two cups. She sat down opposite him and watched him out of demurely lowered eyelids, letting her gaze trail along the lean, smooth lines of his body, the tired planes of his tanned face.

"All right," he said abruptly. "You want togetherness, we'll have togetherness. Why don't you answer a few questions, dear wife? Think you can do that?"

"I doubt it. I don't have any memories."

"The convenient amnesia. I guess it must be catching—I keep forgetting that you lost your memory."

He was in a foul mood, she thought. Obviously the wrong moment for improving their relationship. She rose, but his hand shot out, clamping around her wrist, and she slopped her mug of coffee. He didn't release her, and she refused to sit. She stood there, staring down at him, wishing it gave her even the slightest advantage. It didn't.

"So tell me, Molly dear. Are you still insisting someone pushed you down the cellar hole?" he asked in a silken voice. Despite the firmness of his grip, his thumb was absently stroking the tender inside of her wrist.

"It was the truth."

"And you're such a great expert on the truth, aren't you? What happened the night you left here?"

Damn him, she thought, wishing she could break free. She knew if she tugged again it would just end up in an undignified struggle. "I don't remember," she said stubbornly.

"And you expect me to believe this miraculous case of amnesia? This incredibly convenient memory loss that lets you off the hook, as usual."

"Actually, I expect nothing from you," she said in a cool voice.

"That's wise. Because that's what you're likely to get."

"How nice that we've got that settled. Would you like to let me go?" She asked in her most matter-of-fact tone. It still took on the subtext of a cosmic question. Would he let her go? When?

"Don't you have any questions you want to ask me?" he said lazily. "Since you've been so extraordinarily frank this morning, why don't I return the favor?"

"What would you do if I was pregnant?"

It worked. He dropped her wrist as if burned, and the winter blue of his eyes turned to ice.

"I wouldn't give a damn," he said after a moment. "Unless you tried to pass it off as mine. You wouldn't get very far with that, so I suggest you don't even try. Are you?"

"Am I what? Pregnant? Or trying to pass the child off as yours?"

"Either one."

"Neither one," she said pertly. Not a complete lie. She didn't *know* that she was pregnant—she was just guessing. "I was just daydreaming."

"More like a nightmare if you ask me," he snapped.

"You don't like children?"

"I like children. I don't like you."

To her horror she could feel tears start in her eyes. And it seemed to horrify him just as much, for he rose, suddenly contrite. "Molly, I..."

Before he could finish she had run from the room, anywhere to keep him from seeing her appalling weakness. She couldn't even curse him for a thoughtless bastard; his final softening had precluded that.

Perhaps it was all a lost cause, she told herself tearfully when she reached the haven of her room. She would be much better off if she did keep out of his way. He had told her to, time and time again, and she hadn't listened, stubbornly seeking him out. Looking for something. A faint sign of approval, or even affection?

She knew perfectly well she wanted more than that. And she would never get it—she'd learned that in another lifetime, and that knowledge stayed with her, even as her memory eluded her.

If she had any sense at all she would just stay in her room, passing the time as best she could until this period of waiting was over.

Unless she was pregnant. The thought came unbidden, and resolutely she pushed it away. That was one problem she would not worry about until she had to. But the period of time before her doctor's appointment stretched before her as a yawning abyss.

MUFFINS. She'd brought him muffins and coffee, a peace offering, and he'd thrown them back in her face. He didn't want peace offerings from her. He didn't want her sweet and shy, looking up at him as if she were sixteen again and he was everything she'd ever wanted.

He didn't want to believe in her again. Didn't want to be seduced by her green-blue eyes and her hurt innocence. She wasn't innocent, and she wasn't hurt. And whatever it was she wanted from him, it couldn't be something he was willing to give.

Pregnant. What a twisted, horrible idea. Fortunately he knew she couldn't be. They'd run every test known to man on her while she was unconscious in the hospital, including a pregnancy test. There was no way she could be carrying somebody's bastard. She deserved his contempt for even thinking she could pull off a stunt like that.

But still, she never used to cry. When she'd looked at him, tears filling her eyes, he'd known a shaft of pain, sharp and deep, and he'd wanted to touch her, pull her into his arms, soothe and kiss her.

Damn her. And damn him.

He shoved himself away from the desk and headed outside. He needed to get away from here, and from her. Just until he could get his crazy, irrational yearning under control.

He wanted to believe her. That was the craziest part of it all. He wanted to trust her one more time.

He was a fool.

There was no future for them. She'd leave, and he'd get on with his life. Why couldn't he get that through his stubborn brain?

Of course, what if he was dead wrong? What if she was telling the truth, about her amnesia, about everything? She might really be in danger.

No. That was too much to contemplate. She was

a tramp, a scheming little liar, and if he started believing in her again he deserved everything he got.

He'd made that mistake once before. He wouldn't make it again.

SOME PROJECT, Molly decided, was necessary if she was to survive the next twenty-four hours. There was no way she could manage to get a home pregnancy test kit without a lot of explanations, explanations she wasn't willing to make. If she was going to confine herself to her room, then she needed to do something about making it livable again.

She began clearing the dresser drawers of their meager contents. The mountain of purchases she had made a few days before had been swallowed up in the massive piece of furniture, and she was finished in next to no time. She piled the clothing on the shelves in the similarly bare closet, then began clearing off the tops of dressers, tables and night stands. Half of the junk she threw out, the rest went into the closet with the clothing. She stripped the bed and carried the dirty linen down to the kitchen and Mrs. Morse.

"What in the world is all that?" Mrs. Morse cried, brandishing a spatula.

"Laundry," she said briefly. "Could you get Ben and someone else to help me move furniture today? I've decided something has to be done about my room."

"And what furniture were you planning to put in its place?" she demanded. "I can't take another day off right now to go shopping."

"I want all my furniture from the attic," she answered her, helping herself to another cup of coffee. "I don't care what happens to the junk in my room—we can throw it out for all I care. I just want the room to look as it used to."

Her stern face softened. "Well, I've got no quarrel with that. It just about broke my heart when you did that to your pretty little room. All those fancy drapes and everything—they don't belong in a house like this. I'm just glad Patrick put his foot down when you wanted to tear up the old oak flooring."

"So am I," she said in a subdued voice.

"Go on ahead, then, dearie. I'll get you some breakfast. Coffee and muffins aren't enough to keep a body going. And next time you get up early, remember to turn off the oven when you've finished using it."

"Did I forget?" She blushed faintly, as if caught doing something naughty. "I'll try to remember next time."

"See that you do. Now sit down and I'll be with you in a minute."

Ben arrived a few minutes later, accompanied by Toby. "Just the people we want to see!" Mrs. Morse greeted them as they entered. "Molly needs some furniture moved—do you think two big strong men like you could take care of it?"

"I'd be glad to." Ben smiled, and Molly thought to herself that he surely didn't hold her responsible for hitting him on the head the night of the fire. "How about it, Toby?"

"Certainly." He smiled at her engagingly, his

clear eyes warm and intense. "I was just looking for
someone to go riding with me, but Patrick seems to
have taken off. If Molly will take his place when
we're done then I'm your man."

She looked out at the dark and drizzly sky. "It's
hardly the weather for it, is it?" She couldn't imagine why she'd feel the slightest hesitation, but she
did.

"Oh, the weather will clear up, my word as a
gentleman," he said solemnly.

She was being ridiculously paranoid, and she
knew it. "Of course I'll go riding with you," she
said suddenly, ashamed of her doubts. "I've just
been waiting for someone to ask." And if she waited
for her husband, she thought, she'd wait until hell
froze over. She rose and brought her dishes over to
the sink, suddenly aware of Mrs. Morse's subtle air
of disapproval. "Follow me and I'll show you the
furniture."

Within twenty minutes the room was stripped of
every piece of furniture, and only the rug and drapes
remained. She sent Ben and Toby off with their firm
promises to return a couple of hours later for the
second installment, and, armed with some tools she
had purloined from Patrick's tool shed, she set to
work ripping up the carpet.

It had been glued down around the corners, and
the residue was a nasty, sticky mess, requiring repeated scrapings, rubbings, and washings. But by
lunchtime she had the soft, downy stuff dumped in
the middle of the floor with the satin curtains and

valances piled on top, and her room was beginning to look more like it should.

She dragged the stuff out into the hall and down the two little steps to the attic door. Dumping it in one corner, she stood back to take a closer look at her old furniture. And then she noticed what she hadn't seen before. One of the drawers in the mahogany chest was partly open, and inside was a dried bouquet, the yellow roses faded and dead. And somewhere inside a warning bell rang. She stared at it for a full five minutes, trying desperately to force her memory to work, closing her eyes and summoning up the past. But it remained out of reach, mocking, teasing.

By two o'clock that afternoon the bedroom was once again as beautiful as it must have been before she married Patrick Winters. The oak flooring shone with the glow only old and lovingly tended wood has, the small kilim rugs setting it off perfectly. The furniture belonged in the room, as that other stuff never had, each old and sturdy piece complementing the others. She climbed up on the huge old bed, a mate to the one in Patrick's room, and stared around her with a sense of accomplishment and satisfaction. If she could put this part of her life back together with just a little hard work, surely the rest of her problems could be dealt with as successfully. Perhaps there was hope after all.

As Toby had predicted, the day had cleared off nicely, and the early spring sun was poking through the clouds with increasing frequency. Toby had provided her with one of his own horses, a sweet-tempered lady named Bess with seemingly not a bad habit in her gentle body. The moment Molly was on her back she felt at home, and she realized that at one time she must have been a decent rider.

Toby confirmed this. "It's good to see you riding again. There was a time, a few years back, when you were scarcely out of the saddle from one day to the next."

"Really?" She wasn't as surprised as she sounded.

"You and Patrick used to go to all the horse shows around, winning half the prizes at the very least." There was a touch of envy in Toby's voice, and she thought she could understand why. He sat his horse a bit like a sack of potatoes, his body stiff and unyielding. He was in perfect control of his spirited roan, but there was an unnaturalness about it, an awkwardness that struck the eye immediately. Clearly Toby had never won any prizes in the show ring.

Despite Molly's proficiency, it took a while to realize that she wasn't completely at ease on Bess's back. There seemed a tension about the horse that she hadn't noticed at first, just a small trace of nerves that communicated itself in the subtlest way. They followed the old road that encircled the farm at a leisurely pace, and Molly tried unsuccessfully to attune herself to the horse's odd mood.

"Let's go into the woods," Toby suggested as they neared the farm again. "There's a spot near the old well that should have some daffodils this time of year."

"We've been out rather a long time," Molly said uneasily, her hindquarters beginning to feel a little sore from the unaccustomed exercise. "Perhaps we should save it for another day."

His face fell absurdly, and she felt a touch of guilt. "But daffodils were always your favorite flower, Molly," he said plaintively. "Please. It would mean a lot to me if I could give you your first daffodil of the year."

She didn't want to encourage his odd crush. He always seemed to be watching her, covertly, his pale eyes strangely intense, and there was a peculiar undercurrent to his behavior that she hadn't been able to define. The thought filled her with such a gnawing discomfort that she failed to notice where they were heading as the trees closed around them.

Suddenly, with no warning whatsoever, Bess gave a shrill, frightened shriek, rearing up wildly, and Molly felt herself sliding. She clawed for the reins, but it was hopeless, and she began to fall, through the air, as the ground rushed up toward her. *The baby,* she thought in sudden desperation, determined to protect something she wasn't sure she believed in.

But it was too late. She was falling, falling, and there was nothing but the winter-hard earth to catch her.

Chapter Ten

She lay on the hard ground, the breath knocked out of her, stunned. She closed her eyes, struggling to breathe, waiting for the pain, the cramping to hit her. Her breath came back in a whoosh, and she held very still, listening to her body, listening to the sound of hooves as Bess took off into the forest. Just a few expected aches and twinges. If she was pregnant, it didn't seem as if she'd done anything to hurt it.

Toby slid from his horse and knelt beside her. "Are you all right?"

Molly shook herself, sitting up slowly. "Fine," she responded after a moment, feeling only slightly dazed. It hadn't been the worst fall, she knew that instinctively, but it had still been oddly unsettling. She struggled to her feet and brushed off the twigs and dirt from her jeans. "And there's Patrick," she said, seeing his tall, lean frame at the far edge of the clearing, unable to keep the relief out of her voice. He was accompanied by Ben, and she waved to show she was all right before turning back to her companion.

Toby was standing there with a large rock in his hand, a troubled expression on his gentle face. "You could have hit your head on this and been killed," he said, dropping the rock back to the wet ground.

She stared at him for a moment, unnerved, still shaken by the fall. "I wouldn't worry, Toby," she said finally in a determinedly light voice. "I seem to have an awfully hard head."

His eyes met hers with a look of sorrow. "I have to tell you this before Patrick gets here, whether you like it or not."

"What is it?" she asked with a trace of annoyance. Patrick was advancing swiftly, his long legs making short work of the distance between them. There was a look of thunderous rage on his face.

"Molly, someone or something spooked that horse."

"What?" she exclaimed, giving him her entire attention now.

"I said that Bess was frightened deliberately. Someone tried to hurt you." He looked frightened, really frightened.

"How could they?" she demanded. "You saddled her, didn't you?"

He nodded. "But I left her in the stables alone when I came to fetch you. Anyone could have tampered with her during that time. A small burr under her blanket that would work its way into her skin after a while, a needle. Anyone who's familiar with horses could have done it."

She didn't want to ask the question, but there was no avoiding it. "Who was in the stable when you left?"

"Patrick," he said in a hushed voice.

Panic swept over her, blind and unreasoning. She trusted Patrick—reasonable or not, she was certain he wasn't trying to kill her. But why would Toby lie?

"I don't believe it," she said in a horrified voice. "He wouldn't do anything to hurt me. You must be mistaken."

"It's no mistake, Molly," he said. "I've warned you before. You can't trust anyone, not even your own husband. Let me do the talking when Patrick gets here, all right? He's going to be mad enough that we were even out together without this happening."

"Why should he be mad we went riding?" she asked, startled. "Surely there's no harm in that?"

"You really don't remember him at all, do you?" He shook his head in amazement. "Patrick's always had a dog in the manger attitude about you. He didn't want you for himself, but he was always damned if he would let you go off alone with anyone. And that started years before you were married."

She looked over at Patrick's advancing figure and found a curious lightness inside her, banishing her fear. "How very encouraging," she murmured, half to herself.

"What the hell is going on here?" Patrick demanded when he reached them. "Are you trying to get yourself killed?"

Are you trying to kill me? she almost retorted, but some long-submerged sense of tact kept her silent as Toby tried to explain the situation.

"I thought you knew more about horses, Toby." Patrick's contempt was withering. "After all, you've been around them all your life. Molly hasn't ridden in over a year. You should have put her on one of our horses, not that nerve-racked Bess. And why the hell wasn't she wearing a hard hat?"

"Bess isn't nerve-racked," Toby protested, stung. "She's a fine animal, and Molly always used to beg me to let her ride her."

"That was years ago, when she was in better shape," he said coldly. "And back then I told you no."

"Oh, for God's sake, she's not a child," Toby said in a tense voice, and Molly noticed a faint tremor in his hands. There was something else going on here, something besides the anger over a minor riding accident. Something between them, and it involved her.

"No, but *you're* acting like one, doing a foolish and dangerous thing like that." Patrick's very calm made his stinging words all the more biting, and Toby's face took on a mottled hue.

"Well, I'll leave you to escort your *wife* home." His accent on the word was bitter. "I'll talk to you later, Molly."

"Not for a while, I'm afraid," Patrick told him firmly. "She's going to keep to the house for a few days—I don't like all these accidents that have been happening recently.''

"I don't either," Toby said angrily, and rode off.

Patrick looked down at her from his six feet three inches of male irritation. "Are you satisfied now?" he demanded. "You've managed to come between me and one of my oldest friends." He started walking, and it was with difficulty that she managed to keep up with his long strides.

"*I* came between you?" she echoed angrily. "There was absolutely no call for you to speak that way to him. I think that whatever differences you two have are your own problem and none of my doing. And why aren't I allowed out riding with one of your oldest friends? Do you think he's going to throw me down and have his wicked way with me?"

He stopped and gave her a look of withering contempt. "I would say, judging from your behavior over the past ten months, that he'd be in more danger from you than vice versa." And he walked on.

Once more she had to run to keep up with him. "Then if you hate me so much why don't you let me go?" she demanded. "As long as I give the police my address I can go anywhere I please. I haven't been accused of any crime—I'm just a witness. If I happened to remember anything I saw, that is. So why don't you let me go somewhere and get a quickie divorce and finish this thing once and for all?"

"No." He kept on walking. "You put me through hell for over ten months. I think I owe you six months of hell in return, and I mean to see that you get it."

"Where's Toby?" Mrs. Morse asked cheerily as Molly entered the kitchen alone.

"Gone home," she said morosely, sitting down by the fireplace. "Mrs. Morse, why does Patrick hate me?"

"Oh, now, dearie, he doesn't hate you," she said earnestly, coming to sit beside her with one of her ever-present cups of coffee. "He just doesn't know his own mind, that's all."

"He *does* hate me," she insisted. "And I can't remember what it is I've done to him to deserve it."

"Well, I've always said what's past is over and done with and should be forgiven and forgotten. Unfortunately Patrick's always had a hard time with the forgiving and the forgetting."

"But what makes him so full of hate all the time?" she demanded. "Isn't he ever happy?"

"Well, now, of course he is. But life's never been easy for him. His mother ran off when he was just a kid—died in a car accident a few years later without ever writing or calling. It's not good for a child to feel abandoned, and his father, bless his heart, wasn't the most nurturing soul. He was just as strong-minded as his son, and the two of them fought like cats and dogs, Jared trying to make Patrick do what he wanted, Patrick refusing. It was a real battleground. Finally Patrick just took off in his early twenties, and no one heard from him for years."

"What happened? What brought him back?"

"He never did say, and I doubt he ever will. He went through some bad times, and when he came back he was a changed man. He and his father worked out a kind of truce, and then a couple of years later you showed up. It wasn't until then that he began to be more like his old self, and I thought…well, never mind." She sighed, taking a deep drink of her coffee.

"Why did he marry me?" she asked, unable to keep the forlorn note out of her voice.

"I don't know, sweetie. He treated you like a little sister—took you with him, teased you, talked with you. As for you, it was as clear as day that you were crazy in love with him. Had been since you first came here, sixteen years old and pretty as a picture."

"He told me it was his father's idea."

"It was. He left the estate all tied up to try to get his own way, but then, Jared was that kind of man. But there would have been ways around it. Patrick didn't have to marry you. And I never did figure out why he did."

"It's pretty easy to guess why I did. I was willing to take him on any terms, wasn't I?" she said bitterly, and Mrs. Morse nodded.

"I guess that was so. But it seemed like you changed your mind once the knot was tied. You weren't even friends with Patrick anymore. You became wild and spiteful and selfish, and it was just too much for Patrick to deal with. That, and all the other men."

"Other men?" she repeated, numb.

She shook her head sadly. "Just like his mother. You used to go out and stay all night long with anyone you could find."

It didn't feel right. Perhaps it was just wishful thinking on her part, but Molly couldn't rid herself of the notion that someone, somehow, was lying. "How do you know that?" she demanded.

"Honey, *you* told us! It was no secret—you made darn sure everybody knew exactly what you were doing. And Patrick just shut himself up in that office of his or went off and met Lisa Canning somewhere. I tried to tell you that wasn't the way to win him but you wouldn't listen."

Molly stared into the fireplace, trying to reconcile this image with what she had come to know about herself in the few short days since her...her rebirth. But it wouldn't come into focus, and she wondered what was the truth about her past. Her own instincts? Or other people's sharp memories?

Or neither of them.

MOLLY DIDN'T HAVE much appetite that night. She toyed with the fried chicken and creamed spinach Mrs. Morse brought up to her and barely touched the cheesecake. Uncle Willy brought up a small pitcherful of cranberry juice when he heard she was ill, and it took her most determined efforts to evict him and an oversolicitous Aunt Ermy.

She looked about her in lonely gloom. Even her new surroundings seemed to have palled, and part of her longed to be downstairs, sparring with Patrick over the dinner table, while the rest of her was happy to hide out, away from everyone.

There was something wrong, something very wrong, with this place, and the people, and the stories they were telling her. Something with their image of the past, but there was no way she could refute it.

She could only hold on, one day at a time, and hope she'd have the answer to at least one of her questions by tomorrow.

If she was pregnant there was no way she could leave. Not unless Patrick threw her out.

But if she wasn't, then she'd stayed long enough. She had money, she wasn't charged with any crime. If she got a clean bill of health the next day she was out of here. The answers weren't coming, and whether anyone believed her or not, she was in danger. She was getting out. And she had no intention of looking back.

STUPID BUNGLER! Of course it had been miserable bad luck, Patrick showing up like that. Just a few minutes would have made all the difference. Ah, but that was too often the difference between triumph and disaster. A moment, a whim of fate, and life shifted, defeat beckoned.

But a true visionary never accepted defeat. Not when so much had been accomplished. There was too much at stake, and a whey-faced little thing like Molly Winters wasn't going to get in the way.

The subtle efforts weren't working; neither were the more flagrant attempts. It was time for more drastic measures. There was only a limited amount of time before she remembered.

And when she did, it might be too late for all of them.

Chapter Eleven

It took her over an hour to drag herself out of bed. She was so horribly sick the next morning her entire body felt numb with it, and she alternated between chills and fever, shivering and sweating, until she almost called out for help.

But any cry for help would more likely bring her husband from next door than any one else. She shut her eyes, gritted her teeth, and suffered until the sickness decided to pass.

When she finally got up it was with immense relief that she remembered the doctor's appointment. At least she could diagnose and stop this awful thing. Molly was almost afraid to go to sleep at night, thinking of the pain that awaited her upon waking. She'd have an answer today, even if it might not be the most convenient one.

It all seemed so distant and unlikely. And worst of all, Patrick made it clear there was no way he'd take responsibility for the child. She should have guessed their relationship wouldn't have included sex for a long time. And yet, she could practically feel the heat when he looked at her.

Maybe it was wishful thinking on her part. Maybe she was the tramp everyone said she was. If she was, then there'd be no way of telling what sort of person had fathered her baby. It didn't matter—she still wouldn't want to give it up, she thought stubbornly as she stepped into the shower.

She stood there in the steaming blast of water until she could stand it no longer, then toweled herself off, staring at her body in the mirror. Still the same long legs and flat stomach. Her waist hadn't thickened, her smallish breasts hadn't become tender and swollen. As for missing her period, the surest way of knowing something's wrong, her memory had only been alive for five days. Her body was as mute to her questions as her mind.

She dressed warmly and femininely, in one of the long rayon skirts she had bought and a thick knit sweater. She supposed it was some hidden maternal instinct that made her change from pants to dresses as she contemplated motherhood. She looked at the clock, and noticed with surprise that it was almost noon. She must have needed the extra sleep.

"Well, well, aren't you charming-looking this morning," Lisa Canning's voice greeted Molly as she walked into the kitchen. Molly turned around without a word and headed out, but Patrick appeared out of nowhere, halting her escape.

"Where do you think you're going?" he demanded.

She deliberately misunderstood him. "To the doctor's," she said defiantly.

He raised an eyebrow, and much as she didn't want to, she couldn't avoid noticing the beauty of the man, a beauty that had the power to move her just as his usual contempt pushed her away.

"Well, you aren't going immediately, are you? Come in and have some lunch."

She looked up at him with suspicion of this new affability. "I'm not hungry," she said mutinously.

"Too bad." One strong hand went under her arm and she was brought back into the kitchen feeling like a fish caught on a hook.

Lisa smiled at them both with that cool assurance she had in abundance. "There you are, Patrick. I wondered how long it would take you to tear yourself away from your books. And your little wife too. Did I tell you, Molly dear, how charmingly girlish that little outfit is? So country." She smiled sweetly, and Molly glowered at her in return, yanking her arm away from Patrick's viselike grip.

"You're only young once," she answered her pointedly, flopping down into the rocking chair by the cold fireplace. "How nice of you to come for lunch, Lisa," she said suddenly. "Where are Aunt Ermy and Uncle Willy? I'm sure they'd be desolated to miss you. Especially since we haven't seen that much of you recently."

Lisa flushed, and it was with surprise that Molly realized that she'd inadvertently scored a hit. So Patrick hadn't been going to see her as often as it appeared. Perhaps that situation wasn't as much of a sure thing as she had supposed.

"They've gone off on a visit," Patrick said glumly, and Molly's eyes met his dark blue ones with a tiny shock. He didn't want Lisa here either. He had forced her in here to protect him. She controlled her wry amusement.

"Really? For how long?"

"Tonight and part of tomorrow." He shrugged. "I'm not really sure."

"But then you and Patrick will be all alone here tonight!" Lisa's violet eyes were round as she put into words the thought that had been preying on Molly's mind for the last few moments. "And it's Mrs. Morse's evening off."

She seemed to know more about the domestic arrangements at Winter's Edge than Molly did. But Molly could afford to be generous. She smiled sweetly. "Oh, that's all right, Lisa. We *are* married, you know."

"I know," she shot back in a low voice, quietly declaring her enmity. She meant to have him, Molly knew, and Patrick just as definitely wanted to avoid her. Molly discovered her mood had improved substantially.

"Patrick, dear." Lisa rose gracefully and put one slim, beringed hand on Patrick's arm. "Do you think we could perhaps go for a ride this afternoon? I have so much I've been longing to talk with you about." Her violet eyes shone in her lovely face, and Molly wondered how any man could withstand her.

"Sorry, Lisa," Patrick said. "I'm taking Molly to the doctor's this afternoon."

"You're what?" Molly said in horror.

"I told Mrs. Morse I'd take you. It's her afternoon off and I might as well take on some of my marital responsibilities."

If Lisa had looked sullen before it was nothing compared to her current expression. Molly would have almost found it entertaining if she weren't so appalled at the thought of Patrick driving her to her pregnancy test.

"I'd rather have Mrs. Morse with me," she said faintly. "It's a female problem."

If she hoped to embarrass him she failed. "That's all right, Molly," he said with callous cheer. "I'm a sensitive New Age kind of guy. I want to be there for you."

And all she could do was swallow her snarl of disbelief.

THE RIDE TO Dr. Turner's neat little clapboard house was short and uncomfortable. Neither of them said a word, and Molly tried to concentrate on the countryside. It was all just vaguely familiar. Things were coming back in tiny little bits and pieces and the feeling was oddly unsettling. Most of the faint traces of memory were brief and unhappy. She could begin to recall a tiny part of her wedding night, though it all came to her from a great distance. She could remember taking off the white dress and crying, crying. But she couldn't remember Patrick by her side, taking her into his arms, drying her tears, comforting

her. And when she tried to force remembrance it
would vanish completely, like a wicked, willful
child playing hide-and-seek.

"Do you want me to come in with you?" Patrick
sounded impatient, and she realized it wasn't the
first time he'd asked the question. They had pulled
up in front of the doctor's office while Molly had
been daydreaming.

"No!" she said with a shriek. "I mean, I'm going
for a...a female exam and..."

"I believe they're called a pelvic exam," he
drawled, and she could feel herself flush with embarrassment. Surely a dedicated wanton couldn't
flush? "You need your birth control updated?"

She lifted her head, fighting past her mortification.
"What do I use for birth control?" she asked curiously.

"I haven't the faintest idea."

That should have given her a clue. But she was
too nervous, doubly so with Patrick watching her,
to think about it. "It shouldn't take long," she said,
sliding out of the passenger seat. "You could come
back in about half an hour."

"I'll be waiting," he said. And for some reason
she didn't find that the slightest bit comforting.

Comfort didn't have much to do with her exam
either. After she was finally maneuvered into that
embarrassing and inelegant position on the exam-
ining table she met the doctor's annoyed face with
innocent trepidation.

"You're here to see me about a possible pregnancy, Mrs. Winters?'' she demanded with the awfulness of a member of the Spanish Inquisition.

Molly nodded mutely. In a moment Dr. Turner drew back.

''That's all,'' she said brusquely. ''You can get dressed. See that she gets a complete series of blood tests run on her, then bring her to my office.'' She started for the door, and Molly sat up, yanking the sheet up over her.

''Am I pregnant?'' she demanded nervously.

Dr. Turner stared at her for one long, incredulous moment. ''In my office,'' she repeated abruptly.

Molly was to remember that look of incredulity as she underwent the nastiness of blood tests and three painful finger-pricks. The nurse was a bloodthirsty butcher who took fiendish delight in probing for her recalcitrant veins. It was a full two and a half hours after she first entered the building, and she was practically in a state of nervous collapse by the time they brought her back to Dr. Turner's office. Molly sat there in the small, paneled room, trying to force an interest in the framed licenses and degrees, the walls of medical texts, bracing herself for the news that could change her life forever.

At least no one had brought Patrick in to hear the news. There was something to be said for good old-fashioned sexist GPs, Molly thought with a trace of gratitude.

Dr. Turner entered the room quickly, and sat down opposite Molly, her head lowered. She was the very image of the old-fashioned country doctor, lined face, tired eyes, and Molly wondered what she

had done to earn her displeasure, or to cause this
sudden...was it embarrassment?

"I hear you've lost your memory?" the doctor
said abruptly, staring out at her from faded blue
eyes.

"That's true," she answered slowly.

"I guess that accounts for it," Dr. Turner said,
half to herself. "You're perfectly recovered from
that fall except for a few bruises."

"I know that." Molly brushed the information
aside. "What I want to know is whether I'm pregnant or not."

The doctor leaned back, a look of sudden amusement crossing her weary face. "Well, now, Mrs.
Winters, virgin birth is not a medical impossibility,
but in your case I think we needn't worry."

Molly stared at her in unblinking shock. "'Virgin
birth'?" she repeated, astonished. "You're telling
me I'm a virgin?"

She nodded. "First one I've seen on a girl over
seventeen in I don't know how long." She chuckled,
then sobered suddenly. "Is there something I should
be treating your husband for?"

"You should know that better than I," she said
bitterly. "Aren't you his doctor?"

"Well, he's never complained, but then, men are
funny about that sort of thing," Dr. Turner reflected.
"They're ashamed of it."

"I doubt that he has any problem in that area,"
Molly answered, thinking of Lisa Canning's smug
self-assurance. "He just doesn't care much for me,
I suppose."

"Could be, could be. I think maybe I better see him anyway." She peered at Molly across the desk. "You tell him to come in next week some time."

"I don't think so," she answered, the idea horrifying her. "We're not on very good terms."

"So I noticed," Dr. Turner said, then wheezed with laughter at her own joke. "Nevertheless, I want to see him anyway. In the meantime we'll see what those blood tests turn up—you look a bit peaked to me. We'll find out what's causing you to toss your cookies, young lady, don't you worry. Though I imagine it's nothing more than stress. We'll call you when we get the results." She dismissed her with a wave of her hand, and there was nothing Molly could do but leave, with one question answered and a million more started.

Patrick was sitting in the waiting room, surrounded by sneezing parents and wailing children. He was large and out of place in that feminine setting, and yet he looked curiously at ease amid the chaos. He rose when she came out, raised an eyebrow inquiringly, and then followed her out into the parking lot.

A light rain had begun to fall. She waited for him to unlock the car, climbing in as she prayed he wouldn't ask her what she'd gone to see Dr. Turner for.

She should have known it would be a waste of time. "So," he said, as he pulled out into the highway, "are you pregnant?"

She glared at him. So much for her illusion that

she'd manage to fool him. "No," she said in a little more than a snarl.

"Just as well. Trying to foist another man's child off on me wouldn't do wonders for our relationship."

"I didn't know we had a relationship," she said in acid tones.

"We don't. Let's keep it that way, shall we? Look on the bright side—we don't have to put up with each other for much longer."

"It's a small comfort," she said bitterly.

She saw him glance over at her. He didn't know where her fury was coming from, and she'd be damned if she'd enlighten him.

They completed the drive back to the farmhouse in brooding silence, and Patrick didn't bother to switch off the engine when he pulled up outside the kitchen door. "I don't need to ask whether you can look out for yourself tonight," he said. "You're good at that. I may not be back for dinner. If you get nervous you can always give Mrs. Morse a call. Just don't bring any of your little playmates over. I'll be back sooner or later and I really wouldn't like to find you trying out whatever Dr. Turner gave you."

"She gave me vitamins," Molly snapped. She wanted to hit him. "And you needn't worry about me. I'm used to being alone."

"I'm not worried about you," he said in a rough voice. And he drove away without another word.

MOLLY SLAMMED THINGS around the kitchen in a fine bad temper. The house was cold and empty, and for the first time she wished that her so-called aunt and uncle hadn't chosen *this* Friday for their visit. Unless they left her here alone on purpose, Molly thought, suddenly frightened. She sipped at the ginger ale she had poured herself, heartily sick of cranberry juice, and stared out the window at the darkening countryside. She had had two near-fatal accidents in the last two days. Rather an uncomfortable coincidence, she thought.

With an athletic grace she hadn't known she possessed, she swung herself up onto the scrubbed counter and sat, lost in reflection as the sun sank lower and lower behind the farm buildings. Perhaps Patrick wouldn't be back at all tonight. Perhaps some hobo would come and finish the job on her and they would find her body in a tangle on the floor. There was something going on here, something she didn't like, and the vague snatches of memory that were coming back to her had taken on an ominous tinge. The night of the fire was slowly coming back. She could remember her absolute fear and horror at the sight of the flames licking their way around the stable, could remember Patrick, his face lit up by the orange-red fire, fighting desperately to get in and free the poor, tortured horses. And there was someone beside her, someone laughing quietly, deep in their throat, at the horror in front of them. And she remembered when she was alone, she ran.

But this wasn't enough to go to Patrick with. For one thing, he wouldn't believe her; for another, she had absolutely no idea of the identity of her companion. It could even have been a woman, for all she knew.

No, there was nothing she could do until more of the past decided to reveal itself. In the meantime she could only wait, and watch out, as Toby had warned her.

She thought back to his gentle concern, knowing she should feel some sort of reassurance that someone cared. But all she could think of was the sharp, strange look in Toby's eyes as he'd warned her about Patrick. His urgency somehow struck her as odd and eerie.

It could have been wishful thinking on her part. She didn't want to think Patrick was capable of hurting her. But what did she really know about him, apart from the fact that half the time he seemed to despise her? He couldn't be the one out to hurt her, could he?

Mrs. Morse thought the sun rose and set with him, but then, she was admittedly prejudiced. And everyone else Molly had met, from Toby to Aunt Ermy to old friend Willy, even to subtle remarks from Lisa Canning, had warned her to beware of her husband.

She'd stupidly refused to listen. She was certainly not being very wise. But as she stared out the window at the coming night she knew she would continue to shut her ears. To trust her heart, even if it made no sense at all.

She finished her drink and jumped down from the high counter. It was past six, and no sign of Patrick. Perhaps he wouldn't return tonight, she told herself, irritation simmering within her at the thought. Perhaps Lisa's arms were too strong a temptation even for such a saint as Patrick Winters. She set the stew on the back burner and started it at a low flame. Such a noble man her husband was. She slammed the oven door. Such a considerate gentleman. She threw a handful of silverware onto the table. Such an excellent, restrained fellow. She kicked savagely at the trash can in her way.

She finally ate a furious and solitary meal at half-past eight. At that point she was beyond rage. She knew that if he came in she would hurl her plate with its scorched meat and vegetables at him without a second thought. It was probably just as well that he was nowhere to be seen.

And then she began to brood. Steadily, as she sat in front of the sputtering logs she had tried to coax into a fire. Beastie appeared at the door and elected to keep her company, and for this small, or actually quite mammoth piece of companionship, she had to be grateful.

Her nerves were on edge. She sat huddled in that great chair, her feet tucked under her, staring over her shoulder every few minutes. The hours passed slowly, so slowly, and she knew her nervousness was pure foolishness. All the doors were locked and bolted; no one could enter without her knowing it. She had no intention of letting her errant husband return to his bed without a few choice words.

She must have dozed off, for the next thing she knew the grandfather clock in the hallway was chiming midnight. She stretched, and rose, some of her pique abated from the uncomfortable little nap.

"I suppose we might as well go to bed, Beastie," she said to her companion, and he seemed to nod his massive head sagely, following her up the stairs. She gave no thought to her husband's possible return. He could find his own way in, she thought savagely. If he bothered to return before daybreak.

She washed, brushed her teeth and changed into one of those flimsy nightgowns before climbing up into the firm confines of her ancient cherry wood bed. She was tired, angry, and troubled, and what she needed more than anything was a good night's sleep.

She fully intended to get it.

PATRICK KNEW just what kind of trouble he'd be in if he went home that night. The house was deserted—no one would be there but Molly. Asleep in her room, her blond hair flowing over the pillow, her mesmerizing eyes closed. As long as he waited until she was thoroughly asleep he'd be safe.

He found he was smiling in grim amusement. It was a strange situation indeed, when a man over thirty was afraid of his child bride. He hadn't thought he was afraid of anything, but Molly scared the hell out of him.

No, it wasn't Molly who scared him. It was the way she made him feel. Like there was a chance for them after all, when he knew only too well that love was a delusion and women were hopelessly fickle.

Hadn't his mother taught him that? Hadn't Molly made certain he'd learned the lesson all over again?

There was no sign of Toby at the small apartment he rented over a nearby stables, a fact which under normal circumstances would have bothered Patrick. Toby was an odd one. He'd known him since they were kids, but Toby had always been a little off center, a little shy, just the slightest bit obsessive.

He had no other friends as far as Patrick knew. No love life whatsoever. So where the hell was he at twelve o'clock at night?

His apartment was locked, or Patrick would have let himself in and made himself at home.

There was nowhere else for him to go.

Well, that wasn't strictly true. He could go to Lisa Canning's, and be sure of a welcome. He'd succumbed a few times, when he was mad, when he was lonely, when he'd had too much to drink to be able to refuse what she so blatantly offered.

But Lisa wasn't what he wanted. He knew what he wanted. She lay sound asleep in her bedroom back at Winter's Edge, and he couldn't have her. Wouldn't have her.

Not if he had any sense of self-preservation. He was going to leave her strictly alone.

If he could.

Chapter Twelve

The door slammed open, ripping Molly from a sound sleep, and the light in the hall streamed in her room, silhouetting the tall, furious figure who stood there.

"What the hell do you mean by locking me out of my own house?" Patrick's voice was dark with anger.

She turned to the little clock beside the bed, trying to squash down her initial panic. Three-thirty. "I assumed you weren't coming home tonight," she answered haughtily, pulling the sheets around her thinly-clad shoulders. "I'm nervous when I'm left alone at night." She switched on the light and met his angry gaze with a cool assurance that matched Lisa Canning's most intimidating stare.

"Oh, but you weren't alone, were you?" he demanded with mock sweetness, coming to stand by the bed. He was even more handsome than usual, the anger and frustration making his deep blue eyes glitter in the dim light. He'd been drinking, not enough to make him drunk, just enough to give him an edge. It should have frightened her, but instead she wanted to reach out and soothe away the angry lines in his forehead. She didn't dare. Besides, she was equally furious.

"What do you mean by that?" she said stonily. "Of course I've been alone. Which is more than I can say for you."

"Then why did I see Toby Pentick's blue car driving away from here as I came in?" he demanded in a voice as cold as ice. "At three o'clock in the morning!"

"You're crazy," she snapped. "There was no one here, and even if there was, it's none of your concern, now is it? It's not as if you have any use for me." She stared at him defiantly, trying to hide the pounding of her senses, the heavy, frightened beating of her heart.

"I suppose he's been with you all afternoon and evening, ever since I left you. No wonder I couldn't find him. I should have known if I left you alone you'd be up to your old tricks. Lisa warned me."

"She certainly did, didn't she?" she said tartly. She felt her mouth curve up in a taunting smile, almost of its own accord. "Why shouldn't Toby spend the night?" she asked him slowly, mockingly. "After all, if my husband spends his night with a lover, why shouldn't I?" So this was how rumors got started, she thought almost absently. By her own destructive mouth.

"I told you I wouldn't have you whoring around any more." His voice was calmer now, almost frightening in its quiet fury. "I meant what I said."

"This dog in the manger attitude is absurd. You don't want me, but no one else can have me, is that it? Well, how are you planning to stop me?" She goaded him, goaded him purposefully. Perhaps she knew what would happen, what she was pushing him toward, perhaps she didn't. Tension and violence were strong in the air, and she rose to meet them, mocking him.

There was something else in the air, something familiar yet foreign, in the sudden stillness of his angry blue eyes, the silky menace of his body that had nothing to do with violence.

"That's the second time in the last minute you've accused me of not wanting you," he said in a slow, mesmerizing voice. "Are you trying to tell me something, Molly?"

Now her fear had suddenly become real. "Listen to me, Patrick," she said urgently, clutching vainly for the covers.

He'd reached down and yanked them away from her. "It's a little too late for modesty, isn't it?" he said with deceptive gentleness, undoing his shirt. "I assume you don't mind if I take up where Toby left off." He pulled the shirt from his jeans. "You've made it clear to me that every man in town has had you. I think it's about time that your husband tried out your talents."

Molly watched him in a daze as he went over and kicked the door shut. He yanked off his shirt, coming closer, and she looked up at him with a fierce panic mixed with an undeniable desire. He was strong, lean, muscled, with just a faint matting of hair on his chest. No wonder she hadn't remembered making love with him. She never had. Never touched him. Never lay in his arms. And she'd wanted to. Quite desperately.

She wanted him now. But not with rage and contempt, not by pushing him so far into anger that he couldn't pull back. "No, Patrick," she whispered helplessly, trying to move back out of his reach. "Not this way."

" 'No, Patrick,' " he mocked. "Why ever not, Molly?" He reached out and caught her arm, pulling her upright toward him. "You've always maintained you liked it rough."

Curse my big mouth, she thought numbly, trying to jerk away, but he reached out and caught her, pulling her against the heat and hardness of him. The feel of his bare skin against her set off new sparks of longing and panic, and she pushed against him, not certain what she wanted. He was too strong, too determined, too furious. He pushed her down on the bed, and a moment later his body covered hers.

She almost gave up fighting then. He put his mouth over hers, and there was no denying the harsh, demanding sensuality of his lips, his tongue, thrusting against her.

He was aroused, angry, and she should have known better than to let her humiliation and anger get the better of her. She should have known better.

If she had any sense she'd tell him no. He might be furious, he might have been drinking, but she knew, instinctively, that all she had to say was no, one more time, and he'd walk away from the bed, from her.

And she didn't want him to do that.

She slid her arms around his neck and kissed him back.

It seemed to startle him. She didn't know whether it was her lack of expertise, or the very fact that she was responding. If he was bent on hurting her, punishing her, he would have pulled away.

But he didn't. His kiss gentled, teased at her lips, teaching her, kissing her with slow, deliberate delight that sent waves of pleasure through her body. There was no longer any question as to what was going to happen, and she wondered if she should tell him the truth. Tell him to be gentle, to go slow, to seduce her, love her.

She said nothing. If he left her now he would never come back, and she had no doubt whatsoever that he would leave. Abandon her to her unwanted purity.

She could feel him, hard against her belly. She could taste the desire and reluctant passion in his kiss, and all she could think was, at least he wants this much from me. And there was no way she was going to keep him from it.

He reached down and fumbled with his belt, one strong hand more than enough to keep her captive in a prison she didn't want to escape. He moved her unresisting legs apart, and then paused, staring down at her from his dark, stormy eyes.

"Tell me to go away," he said, and it was a plea,

a dare, a taunt. "Tell me you don't want me. Tell me no."

He was resting against the center of her, and she'd never felt such heat, such longing, such emptiness in her life. "Yes," she said, clutching at his shoulders, pulling him to her, over her, into her.

He filled her, sinking in deep, and she cried out with the sharp pain of it and then was silent. She thought she could feel the start of surprise in his body, and for a moment he was still. She could hear his breath rasping above her in the darkness, and she was terrified that now he'd pull away. Leave her.

But he didn't. His hands loosed their bruising hold on her wrists and reached up to frame her face, and his mouth gently, lovingly kissed away the tears from her cheeks, her eyes, her mouth. Tears she hadn't even known she'd shed.

Those kisses were a blessing, an apology, a promise, and she could feel the initial panic begin to fade. Heat returned, as he began to move, slowly at first, coaxing her along, bringing her with him, until she was clinging to him, desperately, as he thrust faster, deeper, carrying her to a place of darkness and delight. Everything became lost in a swirl of dizziness, a dizziness that was bringing her closer and closer to something she couldn't quite comprehend. She moved with him, instinctively, and she held him fiercely, wrapping her arms and legs around him as they climbed higher and higher. Until the world and Patrick exploded within her.

When he finally moved she made a soft sound of protest. He left the bed and walked out of the room, and she closed her eyes to let the tears pour down her face, no longer fighting them back.

And then he was back, drawing her trembling, unresisting body into his suddenly tender arms and holding her close against the warmth and strength of him. It felt safe, it felt indelibly right. This was where she'd always wanted to be. This was where she belonged.

When her crying finally halted, he pulled back slightly, just far enough to see her face. "What the hell is going on, Molly?" he asked quietly.

She concentrated with deep interest at his muscled shoulder, too shy to meet his fierce blue gaze. He put one hand under her chin and drew her head up. "I said, what's going on?"

She tried to shrug, but his body was wrapped so tightly, securely around hers that she couldn't. "It seems obvious enough," she answered in a low voice. "I was a virgin."

His other hand moved the curtain of tangled hair from her face. "And all those men, all those stories—they were lies?"

"I suppose they would have to be. I don't remember." She shut her eyes in exhaustion and moved closer still, pressing her body against his, instinctively, as if searching for warmth and comfort.

"Don't do that," he said sharply, making no effort to move away. She laid her head against his chest, aware of the sudden response in him, exulting in it. She moved her face, pressing her mouth against his shoulder, and the pulse seemed to jump beneath his smooth flesh.

As if against his will his hands moved over her body, caressing her, healing her, soothing away the battered and bruised feelings and replacing them with rapidly escalating need. He ducked his head down, and almost involuntarily, his mouth found hers, and she came alive under his skillful touch. She lay beneath him, trembling with delight as his hungry mouth covered her breasts, his hands inciting feelings she had never imagined she could possess.

And when he entered her this time she couldn't restrain a sigh of pleasure, holding him fiercely, arching against him. And this time it was so beautiful she wept. And this time, when he exploded within her, she was ready too, and through a daze she heard their voices cry out together.

WHEN MOLLY AWOKE he was gone, and she was alone among the tumbled and stained sheets. Sunlight was pouring in the windows, and she could hear Aunt Ermy's magnificent bellow through the thick stone walls. She must have returned early, Molly thought, reaching out for the discarded blankets and covering her pleasured body lazily. And not a minute too soon.

"Why are you still in bed?" Aunt Ermy demanded from the doorway. She was a symphony in peach crepe. It wasn't her color.

"Don't you knock?" Molly countered mildly, snuggling down into the bed, in the meantime taking a surreptitious glance around the room to see if there was any telltale evidence of Patrick's presence last night. Except for the condition of the sheets there was none, and she almost wondered if she had dreamed it. Dreamed the feel of his warm, smooth skin beneath her hands. His mouth on her breast, his body, thrusting, pulsing....

She turned back to Aunt Ermy's suspicious gaze. "I was tired," she said vaguely.

Aunt Ermy edged into the room, her steely eyes raking over the disordered condition of the covers. Molly was obsessed with the atmosphere of passionate lovemaking that permeated the room, and she wondered that Aunt Ermy could be impervious to it. She obviously could tell something was different but she couldn't quite tell what. She watched Molly out of uncertain little eyes, moving closer, and it took all Molly's strength of will not to scramble away from her.

"Are you all right, my dear?" she inquired in an oozing tone. "You look overwrought. Are you sure you had enough sleep? You might even be a bit feverish. Your eyes are bright and your cheeks are flushed."

No wonder, Molly thought, feeling the color deepen on her exposed skin. She kept her expression determinedly vague. "I'm fine, Aunt Ermy. If anything, I've had too much sleep."

"Well, you needn't be afraid your husband's going to bother you." She sniffed in distaste at the mention of Patrick. "He went off early this morning, leaving absolutely no word with either Willy or me.

According to his beloved Mrs. Morse he won't be back for a day or two."

Molly grew cold inside. "How nice," she said woodenly. She felt as if she'd been slapped in the face. Aunt Ermy's next malicious words made it even worse.

"I thought you should know. And apparently Lisa Canning's gone visiting." She moved a little further into the room, her massive front heaving with spurious indignation, her nose wrinkled in rage. "I think it's a shame and a scandal, the way that man treats you. After all, he should leave you with some pride." A sly smile cracked her powdered and rouged face. "But then," she cast a speaking glance around the room, "you at least have been able to find your own sources of entertainment, haven't you, my dear?"

So the atmosphere of the room hadn't escaped her spiteful eye. But naturally, she assumed Molly had brought a lover up here.

"By the way, Molly, Toby's coming over for lunch," she added meaningfully as she started out the door. "I thought you might want to dress." The door shut behind her majestic figure and Molly was left alone with her hurt and humiliation.

She leaned back against the pillows, pulling the sheet up to her neck as she contemplated her future. Last night had changed her world.

Yet last night had meant nothing to him. He'd simply taken pity on the love-starved teenager who'd always worshiped him.

Except that last night he'd known perfectly well

that she was no longer a teenager, and he presumed that she was far from love-starved.

Except when it came to Patrick, she always would be. Love-starved, adolescent, and bereft.

She climbed slowly out of bed. While she filled the tub she stripped the bed, hiding the stained sheets in her mammoth, empty closet. She didn't feel like sharing last night with anyone, even Mrs. Morse or whoever did the laundry. Obviously, as far as Patrick was concerned, it hadn't happened, and that would be her attitude as well. Things would go on as before, they would get their divorce, and then he could marry whomever he chose. After all, hadn't she heard that men feel differently about these things? What seemed like an act of love for a woman could be merely scratching an itch for a man. His itch was thoroughly scratched after last night. And she thought that now she finally, truly hated him.

She lay in the tub and soaked for fully three quarters of an hour, trying to wash away some of the stain from last night. She should have known it would be useless. Perhaps it was better that he left. Or perhaps she was imagining all sorts of problems where none existed. But couldn't he at least have said goodbye to her?

When she arrived in the kitchen Toby was waiting. He was silhouetted against the window, and for one, brief, joyous moment she'd thought he was Patrick. And then he turned, his light, intense eyes watching her with an odd stillness, and it was all she could do to hide her disappointment.

She greeted him with lukewarm pleasure. "How are you this morning, Toby?" At that moment she was heartily sick of the whole male half of the species.

"Afternoon," he corrected, smiling. "I'm fine. You're looking absolutely beautiful, Molly."

She heard a snort from the corner, and Mrs. Morse hovered into view. "Patrick said he'd be back sometime tomorrow," she said loudly, determined to bring the specter of Molly's husband into the conversation before Toby could get any ideas. "He had some business to attend to, some things to check up on. He said you were to stay close to home, Molly." The look she cast Toby was one of pure dislike, and Molly glanced at her in surprise. Toby was one of the most innocuous human beings she'd met since she'd returned to Winter's Edge.

"Did he?" she said coolly, angry at the arrogant manner of her absent husband's orders. "We'll see." She wandered over and poured herself some coffee, noting with sort of an anguished longing the unaccustomed stiffness in her hips.

"And Dr. Turner's office called." Mrs. Morse was determined. "The results of your tests are in. She said it wasn't what you thought."

"So soon?" She picked up a still warm muffin and bit into it.

"She said she wanted you to come in and see her right away." Molly couldn't miss the note of worry in her voice. "I told her Patrick took the Mercedes and wouldn't be back until tomorrow. The van's out of commission."

"I can take you," Toby offered eagerly, and Mrs. Morse glared at him, slamming a pan down on the wooden counter.

"She said you should call her as soon as you wake up."

"All right," Molly agreed, strolling out of the room into Patrick's office, trying to still the sudden spurt of fear that filled her. She had cancer, she thought dismally, or some fatally crippling disease. And for some odd reason, this was the first morning she hadn't been sick in days. Perhaps sex agrees with me, she thought bitterly, dialing the doctor's number. Perhaps it was a case of terminal lust.

"Mrs. Winters?" She recognized the gruff voice at the other end of the line. "I need you to come in and talk with me today. We've got the results of your blood tests and it's serious. Very serious indeed."

"Really?" Molly replied in a wooden voice. "I'm afraid I can't make it in. My husband's taken the only working car. You'll have to tell me over the phone. Have I got cancer?"

"Certainly not. Perhaps Mrs. Morse could drive you in."

"I told you I couldn't make it," she said, anxiety making her angry. "What's going on? If I'm dying of some strange disease you might as well tell me. At this point I really don't give a damn."

Dr. Turner took a deep breath at the other end. "Mrs. Winters, has anyone else in the house been troubled with nausea recently?"

"Not that I know of. Why, is it communicable?"

"I'm afraid, Mrs. Winters, that you are suffering from arsenic poisoning."

"What?" Molly let out a shriek, then lowered her voice to a conspirator's whisper. "Arsenic?"

"That's right. There can be no doubt of it. Clear traces were found in your bloodstream. Not enough to kill you, just enough to make you quite ill. And of course, over a long period of time it could prove quite dangerous."

"I'm sure it could," she replied numbly, sinking down in the well-worn leather chair in shock.

"I've notified the police, as I'm required to do in cases of this sort. In the meantime, I suggest you only eat what everyone else is eating, and preferably fix your own meals."

She managed to stir herself long enough to protest. "Mrs. Morse wouldn't hurt me!"

"I'm not saying she would," Dr. Turner said patiently. "I'm just saying you should watch out. I expect the police should be out sometime in the afternoon—in the meantime, sit tight and don't worry."

"Don't worry," she echoed, leaning back in shock and the first stirrings of justifiable outrage. "Hell and damnation!"

Chapter Thirteen

He had considered going out and getting thoroughly drunk. However, Patrick had never made a habit of blotting out his memories with alcohol, and six o'clock in the morning wasn't the time to start. While part of him wanted to forget everything that happened the night before, from the moment he'd let his fury give him just enough excuse to enter her bedroom in the middle of the night, until the moment he left her, lying there, sound asleep, the saltwater tracks of dried tears on her pale face, her lips swollen from his mouth, her face flushed and absurdly happy in sleep.

Why the hell had he touched her?

And even more important, why had she lied to him?

If he'd known, he would have been even more determined to keep away from her, though right now he was so angry and twisted up inside that he wasn't quite sure why. After all, he'd married her. They'd entered into a sensible, business arrangement, based on mutual affection and good judgment, and it had turned drastically wrong even before their wedding day.

They'd never discussed just how much of a marriage it was going to be, and he'd assumed that sooner or later they'd get around to sex. To make those grandchildren his father had wanted so damned much.

But as things had gone from bad to worse, and she'd flung her lovers and her hatred in his face, his own mixed longing had chilled. He'd always wanted her. But he'd been just as determined not to have her.

And now it was too late. He'd spent a night in her bed, doing at least some of the things he'd dreamed about when he'd had no control of his fantasies. And he wanted to do more.

He wasn't going to. He was getting the hell out of there, long enough to cool down. To come to his senses. To figure out what the hell was going on here.

Because it was finally getting through his thick skull that something was happening around here. Nothing was as it seemed. In the last few hours his life had turned upside down.

If he'd been wrong about Molly he could be wrong about a great many other things. Like whether or not she'd been pushed into the cellar. Like whether someone was really out to hurt her, as she'd insisted.

Something had been nagging at the back of his mind, some hidden scrap of memory. He wasn't going to sit around on his butt and wait to see what happened. He was going out to find a few answers himself. Just to assure himself that she wasn't in any kind of danger.

When he got back maybe he and Molly could come to some sort of amicable agreement. She could go where she wanted, do what she wanted.

Anything to get his peace of mind back.

And by the time spring rolled around he probably wouldn't even think about her more than once a day.

All day long.

WHEN MOLLY RETURNED to the kitchen she looked at the inhabitants with new eyes. Mrs. Morse was cleaning with a violence, her stern and spare body radiating disapproval. Toby was staring out the window, an odd, abstracted expression on his face, the sunlight reflecting off his wire-rimmed glasses, and Uncle Willy had just come down, hung over as usual, the orange hair combed with its usual finicky neatness, his eyes pale and bloodshot and weary.

"Well, well, Molly," he murmured as he poured a cup of Mrs. Morse's excellent coffee. "You're looking absolutely stunning this morning."

"Afternoon," she said absently, staring at all of them in turn.

"I've already told her so," Toby announced in a playful voice that still held a slightly possessive edge.

Uncle Willy thumped Toby on the back. "Sly young dog," he said approvingly. "Don't miss a trick, do you? Ah, well, when I was your age..."

"Where's Aunt Ermy?" Molly broke in suddenly.

"Ermy?" Willy repeated, befuddled. "I don't know, my dear. She should be around somewhere."

Molly drew herself together with a monumental effort. "I believe the police might be coming by later. They'll probably want to have a word with all of you."

The silence was absolute, as the three other inhabitants of the kitchen stared at her in horror that might have been mixed with guilt.

Mrs. Morse spoke first. "You'll not be saying something's happened to Patrick?"

Uncle Willy snorted bravely. "Not him. He's got nine lives, that one has." His face remained a ghastly white, despite the determined smile. "What are you talking about, Molly? Why should the police be coming here?" he demanded. "Have they...have they discovered something new about your accident?"

"I doubt it," Molly said, sipping casually on her cold and bitter-tasting coffee. "I think they want to find out who's been poisoning me."

Uncle Willy's cup slipped out of nerveless fingers and crashed back onto its saucer. He opened his mouth to speak, then closed it again. "Well," he said finally, his normally affected voice high-pitched and squeaky. "Well."

Toby had already moved to her side, laying his soft, gentle hands on hers in tender concern. Hands so different from Patrick's strong, demanding ones. She pulled away firmly. "This isn't true, is it,

Molly?'' His voice was low and impassioned. "If it
is, I swear to God I'll kill him!''

"Now who do you think you're talking about?''
Mrs. Morse demanded in a blaze of fury, slamming
down another pot and marching across the room,
hands on her hips. "You have one hell of a lot of
nerve, my boy, if you think you can come around
here, playing up to your so-called best friend's wife,
and slander him behind his back. Patrick wouldn't
harm a hair on that girl's head, and well she knows
it!''

Apart from breaking her heart, she thought wryly.
"Mrs. Morse is right, Toby," she said aloud.
"What's between Patrick and me is no one else's
concern.''

Mrs. Morse nodded with grim approval. "You listen to her, young man. If I didn't know better I'd
get awfully suspicious of the way you're trying to
throw the blame on Patrick.''

"This is all nonsense." Aunt Ermy spoke sternly
from the kitchen door, her tiny, piglike eyes glisten-
ing avidly. "What's all this about Molly being poisoned?'' She looked at Molly with an expression of
heavy solicitude that was almost believable. "That
was a nasty blow you took on your head, and I think
you must be suffering delusions of persecution along
with your amnesia. Heavens, no one would want to
poison you! Now, you just put that idea out of your
head and we'll call the police and tell them it was
all a mistake.''

"I'd love to do just that, Aunt Ermy, if it weren't
for one simple thing," Molly said in her calmest

voice. "It's Dr. Turner's idea that I'm being poisoned, and it's more than a stray fancy. There was arsenic in my bloodstream."

"Then you took it yourself, for the attention it would bring you," Ermy said flatly, the look in those tiny eyes hostile. "No one in this house would try to kill you. We all love you."

Molly's deadly calm turned into a slicing rage. "Of course you do," she said bitterly. "You're just dripping all over with concern, aren't you? There's something going on here, and if my memory wasn't such a total blank I could figure it out. But I'll remember. Sooner or later it'll come back to me, and I'll have the answers."

Her words hung in the air like a palpable threat. And she found herself wondering if her angry words had just sealed her fate.

THE POLICE ARRIVED a half an hour later. Molly had taken refuge in her bedroom, and when she heard a car pull up she ran to her window, hoping against all possible hope that it was Patrick. She felt more than a twinge of dismay as she recognized her old friend, Lieutenant Ryker, as he climbed out of the gray sedan.

She was downstairs in time to open the door for him. "You're looking a lot better, Mrs. Winters," he greeted her, stepping into the hall and looking around him with calm, professional detachment. That detachment made her uneasy.

"I'm feeling much better," she said with deceptive politeness. "Why are you here? I would have thought the local police could have handled this."

"I'm sure they could have," he answered in his clipped, emotionless voice, "but they decided it was more my concern than theirs. And rightly so. Sergeant Stroup came along to represent their interests."

Molly's eyes flickered over the man standing behind him, recognizing the leering animosity with faint despair. It only needed this, she thought wearily.

"Is your husband here, Mrs. Winters?" Ryker continued smoothly. "I'd like to have a few words with him."

"I'm afraid not. He doesn't even know about this…this poison business. He left here before I woke and I don't think he's expected back until tomorrow."

"And could you tell me where we could get in touch with him?" There was absolutely no reason for her to be bothered by the simple questions. But she was.

"I'm afraid I have no idea," she finally answered, her voice stiff. "Perhaps Mrs. Morse might know. I assume you'll want to talk with her?"

"All in good time, Mrs. Winters, all in good time," he said in that chilling tone. "Suppose you take me to a nice quiet place where we can talk, and we'll get this business over with as quickly and painlessly as possible."

He didn't appear to be the kind of man who wished to avoid causing pain, but there weren't really any options. She led him to Patrick's office to begin one of the most harrowing half hours in her life.

Every answer she gave to his sharply barked out questions, every statement she made, was pulled apart and delved into as if she were on the witness stand. He patently believed not one word she said, yet Dr. Turner's evidence was impossible to refute. Through it all she was conscious of Stroup's smirking, leering presence, his damp, slightly bloodshot eyes lingering over the leather chair she sat in and the antique desk with the same covetous intensity that he directed at her.

She answered Ryker's tersely worded questions calmly and rationally, keeping her voice level, and in the end he was forced to concede defeat. He hadn't been able to make her cry, as he'd all too obviously wanted, and blurt out the truths of all her so-called crimes. She stared across the desk stonily.

"All right, that will be all for now, Mrs. Winters." He leaned back in Patrick's chair affably. "But I suggest you stay close to home for the time being."

"It seems to me that home is about the most dangerous place for me right now," she said in a cool voice. "But I suppose I really have no choice in the matter."

"No, I suppose you don't," he answered. "Could you ask William Winters to come next please, Stroup? I don't think we'll be bothering Mrs. Winters any more today."

Thank God for that, she thought as she left the

room, brushing unshed tears of anger and humiliation from her eyes. The only consolation in the miserable affair was that Willy and Ermy would have to go through the same thing. Though there was always the chance Ryker would behave toward them with at least a trace of charm.

She saw him before he left, his arms full of little bottles and packages, Stroup's beefy arms similarly encumbered. "We'll be leaving now, Mrs. Winters," he said coolly, his colorless eyes distant and unfathomable.

"What are all those?"

"Samples, samples. We want to see how the poison is being administered, if, indeed, it is. According to your information and that of your relatives, these are things only you could have eaten and drunk in the past four days. We should come up with some answers pretty soon."

"And in the meantime…?"

"In the meantime, I'd be careful, if I were you, Mrs. Winters. Very careful."

MOLLY WANDERED into the living room and poured herself a glass of ginger ale. If ever she needed a stiff drink now was the time, and she wondered wistfully when her ban on alcohol would be lifted. There was no one in sight—she thought she could hear a heated discussion in the kitchen, and she had no desire to join in. One of these people was trying to kill her, had tried three times. Once with the poison, twice with her socalled accidental falls. She wondered if Ryker found those accidents suspicious.

He'd been far too quick to dismiss them—doubtless he thought she imagined them as well.

Dinner that night was an uncomfortable affair. Toby stayed and stayed, far longer than anyone wanted him to, watching out of pale, brooding eyes, and helped polish off the roast chicken and tomato casserole Mrs. Morse had fixed. Molly had helped with the dinner preparations.

She didn't for one moment suspect Mrs. Morse. She simply wasn't taking chances on letting any of the food out of her sight for even one moment.

Apparently Lieutenant Ryker hadn't been any more tactful with Aunt Ermy's dignity, for she spent the entire evening in a state of towering indignation. Of all the possible suspects, Molly would have preferred Aunt Ermy to be the guilty one.

Except that the poisoning had begun before Ermy returned home. So had the fall down the cellar hole in the burned-out stable. No, it didn't seem as if Ermintrude was the villain, even if she was patently unlikable.

It seemed forever before Toby was ready to leave. In desperation Molly walked him to the front door. One of her many mistakes. Before she knew what was happening his arms were tight around her and his hot, whiskey-laden breath was in her ear, urging her to do all sorts of things, including leave the house and spend the night with him. The very thought disgusted her, not from an actual dislike of Toby, but more because of her helpless longing for last night and for Patrick. Who'd made love to her, finally, and then left her.

She pushed Toby away with an unnecessary vehemence. "Please, Toby," she said angrily, straightening her clothes.

"Please, Toby," he mimicked bitterly. "You used to care about me. You used to say I was your only real friend. Remember when we'd talk about going away together? Leaving here, leaving Patrick and all those others. I don't know what's happened to you. I'm only trying to help you. I just don't think you should be alone here tonight with them."

"I thought you decided that Patrick was the guilty party," she said. "In that case I'm perfectly safe with Aunt Ermy and Willy."

"There's no way of knowing who's to blame," he said darkly, making a grab at her. She dodged him neatly.

"Listen, Toby, of course you're my friend. I like you very much," she said wearily, backing away from him. "But I'm too tired to play post office in the hall of my husband's house. I think you should go home and go to bed and try to get over this…infatuation or whatever it is."

"It isn't an infatuation. I love you!" he whispered urgently, obviously affronted. "You promised me…"

"Toby, I don't remember," she said, desperation creeping into her voice. "Whatever I said, whatever I did, whatever I promised. I simply don't remember it."

He stared at her, his face shrouded with hurt. Without another word he turned and left, slamming the heavy door shut behind him.

Molly leaned against the door in exhaustion, and if it wasn't for an odd impulse she would have left it at that. But, for some reason she drew back the little curtain beside the door. Toby was standing by his car, staring up at the house, and there was the oddest expression on his face. A look of strange intensity that was illogically frightening.

And then it was gone, and he climbed into his car. It must have been a trick of the light, or a figment of her imagination, Molly told herself, moving back from the window.

But she was unable to shake the eerie feeling that danced over her shoulder blades, as she pictured Toby's face.

THE BITCH WOULD DIE. Not tonight, much as she deserved it. Tomorrow, when there was time to plan.

She'd die in pain, struggling, calling for help. The life would be choked out of her, and no one would come to her rescue. They would find her body the next morning, eyes open and staring. She would be punished.

And she would accept that punishment, that sentence of death, gratefully.

Chapter Fourteen

Molly woke up early the next morning, her stomach calm. Whoever had sprinkled arsenic in her food had obviously thought better of it now that the cat was out of the bag. Unless, of course, her poisoner was simply gone from the house on unexplained business.

The old stone house was silent and still as she tiptoed through the halls, bundled in a warm blue wrapper, her bare feet moving noiselessly on the wooden floors. It was Mrs. Morse's day off, and it was up to Molly to make the coffee and muffins this morning if she expected to have any. As a matter of fact, it was just as well—at least she was safe from an accidental seasoning of rat poison.

The muffins were just out of the oven, the sun was rising higher in the early morning sky, and she was sitting cross-legged on the counter, wiggling her toes in the sunshine when he walked in the door.

He clearly hadn't been expecting to see her so early. He stopped dead, and they stared at each other across the shadowy kitchen with only the dawning light in it. She set down her coffee cup with great care.

"Good morning, Patrick." Her voice was astoundingly even. "When did you get home?"

"Just now." His husky voice sent chills down her spine. He came over to the counter and poured himself a cup of coffee, and his nearness seemed to set off all sorts of reactions inside her, reactions that she wasn't sure if he was quite immune to. And then he spoke.

"I've come to a decision," he said in a flat, unemotional voice. "I'm letting you leave here. You can go anywhere you want while we wait for the divorce to be final. Nevada and Mexico are known for fast divorces—why don't you take a little vacation and speed things up?"

She stared at him in numb surprise. Then, without thinking, she picked up the cast iron muffin tin and hurled it at his head. He dodged it easily, and it fell with a terrible clanging noise, muffins scattering over the slate floor.

Before she had time to move he had caught her wrist in a tight grasp, the long, strong fingers biting into her flesh. There was a fury about him, held strongly in check, that matched and overwhelmed her own anger, and she was suddenly afraid. He looked like a man who had reached the end of his endurance.

"There's been enough of your tantrums around here, Molly," he said in a low, angry voice. He yanked her down from the counter and she stumbled

against him. "Now go pick that up and put it back
where it belongs."

There was no way she could resist, no way she
could defy him. Without a word she did as she was
told. When he finally released her she backed away
from him towards the door, ready for a quick escape
if need be. "You enjoy forcing your will on helpless
women, don't you?"

He didn't even have the grace to look ashamed.
"The day you're a poor, helpless female will be the
day hell freezes over," he said shortly. "I'll get your
good friend Toby to drive you to the airport this
afternoon."

"I'm not going."

"What the hell do you mean by that?"

"Simply that I'm not going," she answered with
deceptive calm, holding the trump card. "I doubt
I'd be allowed to, anyway. Interesting things have
been happening while you were off with Lisa Canning this time."

He didn't bother to deny it. "What interesting
things?"

"Oh, not much," she said with mock calm.
"Someone's been poisoning me, but apart from that
life has been going on as usual."

"What the hell are you talking about?" There
was no play-acting in the shock that paled his tanned
face. Before she could answer him the telephone
rang harshly through the quiet house.

"It's probably for you," she added offhandedly.
"The police have been trying to reach you since
yesterday morning. I think they suspect you." Ac-

tually she didn't think any such thing; she just wanted to annoy him.

He didn't give her the satisfaction of a response. Without a backward glance he went into his office, shutting the door quietly behind him. She would have felt better if he'd slammed it. She stared after him as she contemplated listening in on the extension, then dismissed the idea. For one thing, it was terribly dishonorable, for another, more important reason, she was afraid she'd get caught. She trudged back to her bedroom and did her own door slamming.

When she returned downstairs she felt a bit braver. She was showered, dressed, armored against the world, against Patrick, against her own vulnerabilities. Ermy and Willy were still asleep—the twin snores coming from their rooms assured her. Patrick's office door was still shut tightly, and she went on into the kitchen for another cup of coffee and to work on the Sunday crossword puzzle, determinedly oblivious to the man just out of sight. Forever out of reach.

A half hour passed, then an hour, before Patrick finally removed himself from his inner sanctum and came to stand before her. His belt came to about eye-level as she looked up from the table, and it was with great concentration that she kept her eyes above rather than below it.

"Molly," he said, and his voice was gentler, "I want to talk with you."

She wasn't going to like this, she thought suddenly. And once more she felt like running, from

Patrick, who'd never loved her, from Winter's Edge. From her own, helpless longing.

But running was no longer an option.

"All right," she said, bracing herself.

He pulled out a chair, apparently at a loss for words. He's going to say something about that night, she thought in relief. It's going to be all right.

But she was wrong. "That was Lieutenant Ryker on the phone a while ago. You're right, there's no question of your leaving right now."

She nodded, saying nothing, determined to hide the hurt in her eyes.

"They've found out something else, Molly. They found out who the man was. The one in the car with you."

She stared at him blankly. "I thought they knew who he was. A small-time crook named George Andrews."

He winced. "That was one of his names. I can't believe it took them so damned long to come up with a real one, but then, he was always good at covering his tracks. He was born Gregory Anderson." He waited for a response, one she was unable to give.

"Should this mean something to me?" she asked. "If you want it to then I'm afraid you'll have to explain the connection."

"Gregory Anderson was your father."

She took a deep, shaky breath, shocked. "Really? I thought you told me he was dead."

"He is now," Patrick said sharply. "Don't you care at all?"

She stared at him openly. "I don't remember him. How many times must I tell you before you get it through your head—I don't remember. I must have known he was my father. Otherwise why would I have been with him? But I don't remember anything about it." Her voice rose uncontrollably. "How many times must I say it? I don't remember, I don't remember, I don't remember!" She bit down on her lip to stop the hysteria that threatened to overwhelm her, and she turned away, unable to look at him any longer.

"All right," he said after a long moment. "I suppose I have to believe you." His face was unreadable. "The question of the money was also explained. It was yours, withdrawn from your various accounts, all legal and proper." He gave her a cool look. "It's been redeposited, by the way."

"But why?" she echoed, puzzled. "What did I want with that much money?"

"You're the only one who can answer that, if you choose to."

"Damn you, Patrick, I..."

"All right, if you *could,*" he amended.

"You know what it sounds like to me?" she said after a long moment. "It sounds like blackmail money."

"What could you have done to warrant blackmail that we didn't already know about?" His voice was cynical.

She opened her mouth to protest, then shut it again. It would be useless to argue further. He'd believe what he wanted to believe.

He rose, his tall body towering over her, and she shivered slightly, longing for all sorts of things, longing to simply lean her head against his hip. "Lieutenant Ryker said he'd keep in touch. He also found out how you were being poisoned."

"So he believes me?" she said in a defeated voice. "Finally. How was it done?"

"It was in the cranberry juice. No one but you touches the stuff, so whoever put it there knew you'd be the only one likely to drink it." His face was impassive. "I'll go get rid of it."

"Why don't you have some yourself?" she muttered sweetly, low enough so he couldn't hear as he started out the door. He stopped and turned for a moment, and she thought perhaps he had heard her after all.

But he hadn't. "About Friday night," he began, his voice huskier than usual.

She froze, and she could feel her face draining of color. "Yes?" she said without looking at him, very busy with the newspaper.

"I should have never come in your room. I shouldn't have lost my temper, and I certainly shouldn't have touched you, considering our situation. It won't happen again."

He left the room before she could answer, and she stared unseeing at the crossword puzzle in front of her. The pencil point broke.

"Oh, won't it?" she said to herself softly, determinedly. "We'll see about that."

WHEN ERMY and old friend Willy arrived downstairs, somewhere between noon and one, Molly was in the midst of luncheon preparation, and she turned a deaf ear on their requests for eggs and sausage.

"It's lunch time," she said flatly. "And I'm not used to cooking. You'll have to make do with coffee and muffins until I'm finished, which should be in about an hour." She pushed a stray strand of hair off her sweating brow.

"Now, Molly, dear, you don't know how to cook," Aunt Ermy said heavily. "If you'll simply let me take over I'm sure I'd do a much more competent job. And then Willy and I could have our breakfast. Surely you must realize that you're being unreasonable?"

"Am I?" She looked at them coolly. "Well, this time you're going to have to humor me. I intend to cook all the meals that Mrs. Morse isn't here for." She smiled sweetly, turning back to her labors. There was a moment of annoyed silence, and then Aunt Ermy stomped into the dining room.

What with clearing off their messy dishes, resetting the crumb-strewn table, and dashing back and forth between recipe book and stove, the lunch was more than an hour in coming, a fact which bothered her not one bit. When it was almost ready she started out the back door to look for Patrick, who'd disappeared somewhere in the vicinity of the barns.

Molly saw her before she came up to him. Lisa Canning was dressed all in pale lilac, the pants fitting her perfect legs with nary a bulge or wrinkle, a scarf tied carelessly around her throat. Molly ducked behind some hay bales, then edged closer, eavesdropping shamelessly on their conversation. It was wrong. It was an invasion of privacy. It was irresistible.

"Where were you yesterday?" she was asking in her low, attractive voice. "I waited and waited. I thought we had decided we were going to meet."

Patrick's withdrawal was clear even before he spoke. "I had things to think about, Lisa," he answered shortly, with less sympathy than he usually seemed to direct toward her.

"What things?" she demanded, pressing her lithe body closer to him until Molly wanted to scream. "I thought we'd made all the decisions that had to be made."

"You made the decisions, Lisa," he answered. "I neither agreed nor disagreed."

Lisa moved away then, and from Molly's vantage point she could see the anger in her beautiful eyes. "I never thought you'd be like this." Her voice was petulant. "I'm not used to being jilted, Pat. If that's what you're doing. Ever since that baby-faced little bitch of a wife came back you've been making excuses for not seeing me. It wasn't like that before she went away." She moved back to him, her slender body swaying seductively. "Come on, Pat. You don't love her. You're just piqued that she'd have nothing to do with you, and you know it. She's a child, darling, and a spoiled one at that. Why don't you send her off to get a divorce and put an end to this charade? And then we'd have time to learn whether there might be something for us? Don't you think we deserve it?"

He pulled away from her. "I suppose it would be too much to ask if you'd leave me alone?" he asked coolly.

"Yes, it is! You can't do this to me, playing the devoted lover one minute, the model husband the next. I want to know where I stand in your life! Are you going to divorce her?"

Molly held her breath, an impossible hope building inside her, but it was useless. "Yes, I'm going to divorce her," he said. "But it doesn't have a damned thing to do with you. Look, Lisa, it's been over a long time, and it wasn't much to begin with. We were both lonely, you and I, but we both know it was a mistake."

She stared up at him. "That brings me to the second question, though it sounds like you already answered it. Are you going to ask me to marry you?"

There was a long pause, and Molly almost felt sorry for her. "Lisa, I couldn't afford you, and well you know it." His voice was suddenly gentle.

She laughed unhappily. "How very flattering of you, Pat. The truth of the matter is that you don't want to marry me. And I think, if you were really honest with yourself, you'd admit that you don't want to divorce that unfaithful wife of yours either. There's nothing you'd like better than to play love's young dream with her, regardless of the fact that she's ten years younger than you and she's cheated on you with every man she could lay her greedy little hands on."

"She doesn't have anything to do with you and me, and I'm not about to discuss her with you."

"But there is no you and me. There hasn't been really, since before you married her. And there never will be."

"No," he said with great finality. "There never will be."

She stared at him for a moment longer, then she reached up and ran her hand along Patrick's face with a longing gesture. "It's a shame, darling," she murmured. "It could have been marvelous." She sauntered out the door with more self-assurance than Molly knew she possessed, and she felt a moment's compassion for the woman.

Without another word Patrick turned and started toward the door. Molly ducked back among the bales of hay, but she needn't have bothered. His mind was on other things, and, as she watched his closed face, she wondered what she had done to him, why things had gone so terribly wrong in that shadowy past, and she could have wept with frustration and nameless guilt.

It took her a moment to compose herself. She couldn't very well spend the rest of the day out in the stable, and the conversation she had just overheard was having a belated effect on her. If he didn't want Lisa Canning, then there might, just possibly, be a chance. For the future. For them.

She entered the kitchen close on Patrick's heels, unable to keep a little bounce out of her steps.

"Oh, there you are," she said blandly. "Lunch should be ready. We're eating in the dining room for the time being." She gestured to the table littered with dirty bowls, cutting boards, and cookbooks.

A brief smile lit his forbidding face. "You cooked it?"

"I did, indeed. And very tasty it will be, if I haven't burned it looking for you." She pulled the cast iron skillet out of the oven and noted with satisfaction the golden crust.

"I was in the barn," he said, looking at her curiously and not without suspicion.

"Really?" she said ingenuously. "Well, that's where I should have looked, I suppose. Would you call the others?"

Chapter Fifteen

"What the hell made you decide to wear that dress?" Patrick demanded explosively after a moment of dead silence.

Molly stared down at the white eyelet dress, one of the few pieces of clothing left from her original wardrobe. "You told me I usually dress for dinner. I thought I would tonight. What's wrong with it?" she asked, touching the delicate material. "It's pretty."

Uncle Willy snorted into his drink, and Patrick continued to glower, so it was up to Aunt Ermy to explain the situation.

"That, my dear, was your wedding dress."

It struck no chord of memory. She stared down at it, trying to force some faint glimmer of recognition, but it meant nothing to her. Just a pretty dress.

"I would appreciate it if you'd change, Molly," Patrick said heavily after a moment, and there was pain in his dark blue eyes, a pain she recognized with an unholy pleasure. He couldn't be indifferent to her.

"Yes, my dear. Something in black would be more suitable on today of all days," Aunt Ermy said.

"Why today of all days?" she inquired innocently.

"Because your poor father's death has just been made known to us," she snapped back. "Granted, no one had seen or heard from him for a decade— Patrick's father, rest his saintly soul, assumed poor little Molly was an orphan when he fetched her home here. You'd been staying with some distant cousins, but they no longer had any room for you, so Jared took you in. Such a kindly man, always taking in waifs."

"Yes, wasn't he?" Molly said with a pointed look at Ermy's smug direction.

Ermy, however, was oblivious. "I'm certain Jared would want proper attention paid to your father's death. After all, he was Jared's third cousin. Or something like that. A little more decorum and proper feeling wouldn't hurt you one bit, my girl. Go and change."

Molly smiled sweetly. She knew what she looked like in the dress, and nothing was going to make her take it off. Nothing short of Patrick's strong, clever hands. "I don't think my father would mind," she said coolly. "Now, if you're all finished your drinks you might go into the dining room and I'll bring dinner in."

"Don't you want a drink first, dear?" Uncle

Willy spoke up suddenly from his seat in the corner, his voice surprisingly clear for someone in his usual state of inebriation. "Some of your cranberry juice? You've been working hard all day, I should think you'd deserve a break."

Patrick's eyes met Molly's for a pregnant moment, then he let out a deep breath. "Molly's only drinking Diet Coke nowadays, Uncle Willy," he answered smoothly. "She's been putting on weight."

She considered hitting him, then thought better of it. She glared at him, only to find the expression in his dark blue gaze to be curiously tender. And suddenly she felt sixteen again, in love with the man who always teased her unmercifully. The unbidden memory was like a sharp pain, one that vanished almost as swiftly as it came.

She was in the midst of the tedious job of cleaning up after dinner when Patrick appeared in the doorway. Aunt Ermy and old friend Willy had retired with full stomachs to the living room without offering to help, and she'd somehow managed to use just about every pot and pan in the well-equipped kitchen. The place was a disaster area, and it took her a moment to realize she was no longer alone. She looked at him questioningly, up to her elbows in grease and soap.

He put his strong, beautifully shaped hands on her waist and pulled her gently away from the sink. At his touch she stiffened, then willed herself to relax. She wondered idly whether he was going to kiss her, but after a moment he released her, and she had no choice but to step back.

"You put the dishes in the dishwasher," he said quietly, "and I'll finish these."

She stood motionless for a moment, watching him as he started to work. Then she began clearing the table, slowly, so as to savor every moment of this odd harmony between them. She would brush her body against his as she bent to load the dishwasher, and each time she did so she could feel the little quiver that ran through his body. At least, she thought with satisfaction, she was having the same effect on him that he was having on her.

It was an odd, ritualistic sort of dance they did, their hands touching as they both reached for things at the same time, his body glancing against hers as he moved around the kitchen. The tension in the room built, slowly at first, and the air grew warmer, tighter, darker, until her hands were trembling with pain and love and desire and hurt all rolled into one mass of emotions, the foremost of which was desire. She didn't want to think about what she felt for him. She wasn't ready to admit that she loved him completely and forever, the way a woman should love a man. She didn't know him well enough in this new life to make any such rash statement. But the more she edged away from such a commitment, the more she knew deep down that it was true. Had always been true, since the first moment she'd seen him, back in the forgotten past.

Together they cleaned everything in that kitchen: the toaster, the stove top, the counters, the cupboard doors, the sink, the floor, anything to put off the moment when they had to face each other. And then it was spotless, and there was nothing left to do, no way they could postpone acknowledging each other's presence.

They were standing close together, too close, and Molly finally looked up into his eyes, and what she saw there, beneath all the hostility and hurt she had dealt him over the past, was the man she had fallen in love with seven years ago when she was sixteen and he had just come back from his self-imposed exile. The look in his eyes was as hungry and yearning as the feeling in the pit of her stomach, and she wanted, needed him to touch her. To take her. The moment stretched and held.

And then he broke it. "I'm going to work on accounts," he said abruptly, turning from her.

She felt a slap of total despair and rejection. How could he ignore what was between them? "You do that," she said tonelessly. "I think I'll just go up to bed and read a bit. I'm very tired."

"That sounds like a good idea," he said absently. "The weather report said we might have thundershowers tonight. You'd better be prepared—maybe you should take one of Ermy's sleeping pills."

"Why?"

"You're terrified of thunder and lightning," he answered shortly. "I want you to promise me you'll take a sleeping pill. You need a good night's sleep."

She stared at him, wondering about his insistence. Perhaps if she was knocked out then she wouldn't be a temptation to him. That was the last thing she had in mind.

"No, I don't like to take pills," she answered

calmly. "Especially not someone else's. I'll be all right. It seems like such a silly thing to be frightened of."

He hesitated a moment, and she wanted to throw herself into his arms, wantonly, shamelessly. She waited for a sign, a weakening. There was none.

"Well, good night, then," he said after a moment.

"Good night," she answered, not moving. He stood there for a second longer, torn between conflicting emotions. She knew, she just *knew*, he wanted her. But apparently his control over his desires and emotions was much better than hers. He turned and resolutely walked out of the kitchen.

MOLLY COULDN'T get to sleep. For a moment she contemplated taking one of Ermy's proffered sleeping pills, then shut the thought out of her mind. She had to be awake tonight, she thought grimly. He would come to her tonight, she was sure of it. She lay in the wide bed, the light off, listening for footsteps.

Aunt Ermy came up first, her heavy, determined tread unmistakable on the old oak flooring. She paused for a moment beside the door, and Molly could hear her heavy breathing.

"Molly?" Her voice called out softly.

"Yes?"

There was a surprised pause. "Are you sure you wouldn't like a pill? I don't like the sound of that wind."

"I'm sure."

Her footsteps moved on, and a short while later

Uncle Willy's tired, slightly unsteady feet followed hers down the hallway. He didn't bother to stop along the way—he made his way to his bed with single-minded enthusiasm. She lay there in the dark, listening to the ominous sound of the strong April wind rushing through the trees.

And then came the sound she had waited so long for. Patrick's footsteps, firm and resolute, climbing the twisty stairway slowly, reluctantly, perhaps. She lay perfectly still, breathless, waiting, as she fingered the soft white nightgown she wore, its bridal lace. She could hear his footsteps coming closer, closer. And then he too stopped outside her door, and her heart stopped beating for a second, then slammed into action again, faster now. Before she could call out he left, continuing down the hall back to his own bedroom. Molly turned and wept silently into the pillow.

She must have dozed off. There was a flash of lightning in the room, an enormous crack of thunder, and she was sitting bolt upright, trembling with an instinctive fear. She had to stay calm, she told herself shakily. *There's no place to run to this time.*

She lay back reluctantly, shivering slightly, willing herself to go to sleep. So he didn't want her. He'd already tried to make that clear, and she'd been an adolescent fool to ignore it, hoping against hope that her heart was right and her common sense was wrong.

Well, she'd just had a salutary lesson. He was in his own room, he had no interest in her, and the night loomed ahead, long and endless.

She closed her eyes, trying to will herself back to sleep, when she thought she heard a movement by the bed. Before she could reach to turn on the light something loomed over her, something huge and dark and dangerous. Lightning split the sky, illuminating the room, but the creature looming over her seemed huge, faceless, as his hands latched tightly around her neck, pressing, pressing tightly.

She fought, kicking out, her hands beating at his iron strong arms. She couldn't make a sound as the breath was slowly squeezed out of her. She scratched at him in desperate fury, kicking.

The lamp beside the bed toppled over with a resounding crash, and he cursed, a muffled obscenity, in a voice eerily familiar.

And then suddenly she was free, the death-dealing hands had left her, and she was alone in the room, in the darkness, gasping for breath.

She struggled out of bed and turned on the light. Whoever had been in the room had knocked over a chair when he made his escape, and the door to the hallway stood gaping open. She held herself motionless, listening for the sound of escape, but there was nothing but the sound of the storm outside, covering any retreat. And then the thunder crashed again, shaking the ancient stone foundations of the old house, and she let out a shriek of terror, dropped the blanket and ran from her room straight into Patrick's.

She headed blindly for the bed, throwing herself into his arms, sobbing desperately. "Someone just tried to kill me," she said in a hoarse, raw voice. "He came into my room and tried to strangle me!"

He was already sitting up, trying to disengage himself from her panicked, clutching arms. He switched on the light and stared at her in disbelief. "That's impossible," he said flatly, doubting blue eyes narrowed against the sudden light. "You must have had a nightmare."

"I didn't, I swear I didn't!" she cried, hysteria and something else shattering her tenuous control. "Someone came into my room and tried to kill me. Can't you hear it in my voice—I can barely talk. It's true, I swear it! You can go and see for yourself—he knocked over the furniture as he escaped."

"Why did he run? You're hardly formidable enough to fight him off. Why didn't he just finish the job?" Patrick asked flatly.

She stared up at him, pain and fear subsiding into shock. "I don't know," she said numbly.

"You must admit you don't have much of a record for truth telling," he said.

She started to pull away from him, but his hands suddenly tightened on her arms, as if he regretted his harshness. "If you're afraid of the storm, Molly, you just have to say so."

"I'm not..." She started to deny it, but another flash of lightning sparked through the room, followed by a crash of thunder, and she jerked, clutching at him more tightly.

A tentative hand reached out and smoothed her tumbled hair. "I think you must have dreamed it,

Molly," he said, more gently now. "Thunderstorms always affect you that way."

"Why won't you believe me?" she demanded hoarsely.

He sighed, and with surprising tenderness reached down and pulled her into the bed beside him. He leaned over and turned out the light. "Lie down and go to sleep, Molly," he said patiently, slipping down under the covers, for all the world as if that was exactly what he intended to do himself.

In the meantime Molly was making some interesting discoveries. In the first place, Patrick slept naked, and the feel of his warm, smooth skin next to hers was having a predictable effect. She wanted to move closer, to press herself against him, to breathe in the feel and the scent of him.

It was also becoming apparent that she was having the same effect on him.

Lightning lit up the room for a moment, and she shivered and drew closer to the warmth of his body. The thunder followed a moment later, and she could barely resist hiding her head. Tentatively she put her face against his shoulder. His arm came around her waist, almost by its own volition, and he pulled her closer as she snuggled against him, the warm, lean hardness of his body. He put his hand under her chin, moving her head up, and his lips tasted hers, gently, almost wonderingly. With a sigh of pure abandonment she put her arms around his neck and moved closer still.

She couldn't have imagined it could be any better, but amazingly it was. His mouth was soft on hers, tasting, demanding, his hands exploring her body with a tenderness she would never have expected from a man of his temper and passions. He slid the nightgown from her, pulling it up slowly until it came free, and then it was as if he'd finally given himself free rein.

He was everywhere on her body, hands and mouth, tasting, touching, arousing her to a fever pitch she hadn't imagined possible. And when he entered her this time she clung to him, sobbing lightly, wanting more and more of him. She felt she would die if he left her; this sweet, soft dream should go on forever, when he suddenly turned rougher, exciting her in ways she hadn't even known existed, and her fingernails raked his back as she held him, straining with a passion as savage and dark as his own.

And when it was over, when she fell back, panting and warm in her dazed completeness, she still held on to him, determined not to let him leave her, not to let him shut her out.

She fell asleep in his arms, his body wrapped tightly with hers.

Chapter Sixteen

When Molly awoke the next morning he had already left the bed, and she lay calm and contented beneath the covers, watching the sun grow brighter and stronger, waiting for her husband to return. She had almost drifted back into a blissful sleep when the door opened and he came back in, dressed only in his faded blue jeans, his long black curls dripping from the shower onto his strong shoulders. His eyes slid over her lying in his bed, for all the world as if she belonged there, and the same old expression of distrust filled his dark blue gaze.

She couldn't stand it. Without thinking she slipped out of bed and ran across the room to him. Throwing her arms around his neck, she pressed her warm, naked body against his. "Don't look that way, Patrick," she pleaded, with tear-filled eyes. "Whatever I've done, whatever way I've hurt you— that's in the past. I can't change it, I can't even remember it." Reluctantly his dark blue eyes met her intense gaze. "All I can do is love you, Patrick," she said in a quieter tone of voice. "I know that I always have. And I just wish you could accept that and try to trust me. Just a little bit."

"Molly, this is hopeless," he said wearily. But his hands had reached up and caught her arms, holding her against him, his long fingers stroking her skin. "We have too many strikes against us, not the least of which is I'm of a different generation."

"You're ten years older, for heaven's sake!" she snapped, seriously annoyed. "That hardly makes you Methuselah. If you try really hard you should be able to come up with a better excuse than that."

He looked down at her, stroking, stroking. "And what if I don't want to?" he said in a husky, uncertain voice.

She held very still. "Want to what?"

"Don't want to come up with any more excuses."

The tension between them was fragile, tentative, and unbelievably delicate. She almost didn't dare breathe, for fear she'd shatter the possibility in his words. He leaned over and brushed her lips against her eyelids, first one, then the other. Feathered across her cheekbones, danced across her mouth, clung for a moment, then moved on. When he moved back she was dazed, so lost that she couldn't move, couldn't react as he grabbed a shirt and left the room.

He'd kissed her many ways, in many places during the nights she'd spent with him. He knew how to use his mouth, to arouse, to satisfy, to delight.

But he'd never kissed her with love before.

SHE PUT OFF going downstairs for as long as possible, using every speck of hot water the old house possessed, turning on her radio and humming loudly while she moved around her room. She didn't want anything, any noise, any creature, to intrude on the burgeoning hope that was burning inside her. She didn't want to face Patrick in front of Ermy and Willy's knowing eyes, and she didn't want to frighten Patrick away.

So she tried on half a dozen changes of clothing, finally ending up in a huge cotton sweater and faded jeans, put on makeup and then washed it off, tucked her hair in French braids and then ripped them out. It took all her concentration to wipe the smile off her face a mere second before she entered the kitchen.

The sight that met her eyes was enough to depress anyone. Willy was up early and sitting in the corner, looking even paler than his nightly imbibing usually made him, and the carrot-colored strands of hair were disarrayed on his balding skull. Mrs. Morse was slamming pots and pans around in a bad humor, causing Willy to wince dramatically.

"What's wrong with everybody?" she demanded brightly. "It's a beautiful day, the sun is shining. What...?" she noticed that Aunt Ermy was snorting and snuffling and dabbing away at red-rimmed eyes. "What's happened?" she continued in a lower voice.

Aunt Ermy looked up, dislike and disapproval emanating from her tiny, tear-filled eyes. "You're a fine one to ask! Why should you care, spending the night romping around with that man while all the while...all the while..." She dissolved into noisy tears.

Molly could feel the color flood her face as she struggled to remain impassive. "What are you talking about?"

Uncle Willy took over, a look of stern condemnation on his ruddy face. "Your Aunt Ermy was referring to your behavior last night. You left your door standing wide open, my dear. There was no doubt in our minds where you'd gone. Besides which, his bed creaks."

She could feel her color deepen. It had squeaked noisily, rhythmically, most of the night. There'd been other sounds as well, but at least Uncle Willy didn't seem likely to mention them. "I spent the night with my husband," she said, a little too loudly. "I don't know what's so shocking and immoral about that." She poured herself a cup of coffee with a deceptive show of nonchalance. "Surely that's not cause to make you burst into tears?"

"Sometime in the night, my dear Molly," Willy began portentously, "while you were disporting yourself with your husband, Toby Pentick was murdered. Someone cut his throat."

"What?" She sat down abruptly, feeling faint. "That's impossible."

"I'm afraid it's not only possible, it happened, Molly," Mrs. Morse broke in from her stance by the sink. "The police came by not half an hour ago and took Patrick with them. For questioning, they called it." She snorted. "Seems like they found something of his by the body. What you might call circum-

stantial evidence.'' She shook her iron-gray head.
''And now God only knows what's going to happen.''

For a moment Molly couldn't move. It was as if
a dark cloud had hovered over them all, and with
the advent of the thunderstorm, disaster had broken
free. She crossed the room and put her arms around
Mrs. Morse's spare figure, trying to still the sudden
spurt of despair that had shot through her heart.
''He'll be all right, Mrs. Morse,'' she said, not certain if she was trying to reassure the older woman
or herself. ''It's all a stupid mistake, you'll see. He
was with me last night—there was no way he could
have killed Toby. Why in the world should he want
to do such a thing?''

''Jealousy, my dear,'' Willy said from his seat in
the corner in a firm voice. ''He was mad with jealousy over you. Everybody knew it.''

''And you made sure that the police found that
out too, didn't you?'' Mrs. Morse turned on him
wildly. ''You nasty, sponging drunk, ready to stab
a man in the back when he's not looking.''

''Now, now, my dear Mrs. Morse, I was only doing my duty,'' Willy protested mildly, unmoved by
her attack. He rose from his seat. ''You don't seem
well today. This business has upset you—why don't
you take the rest of the day off?''

''I don't have to discuss it with the likes of you
if I do!'' she flared back, turning to Molly. ''As a
matter of fact, I thought I might ask Ben to take me
home after lunch. This has got me all upset—I don't

know whether I'm coming or going. You can manage, can't you?''

"Of course I can,'' she said soothingly, stilling
her own doubts. ''You leave whenever you feel like
it, and I'll give you a call as soon as Patrick gets
back home.''

"You'll be waiting a long time for that,'' Willy
said with a smirk, and Molly nearly threw a pan at
him. Fortunately there was nothing close at hand, so
she had to be content with glaring at him fiercely.

"Willy and I were also planning on leaving this
afternoon,'' Ermy piped up in a watery voice. ''A
short round of visits with our friends the Sturbridges
would get our minds off this distressing business.
We should be back in a couple of days. Unless, of
course, you're afraid to stay alone?'' she hinted
slyly.

"I won't be alone,'' Molly shot back grimly.
"My husband will be here.''

"Of course, he will,'' Willy said in a soothing
voice. ''You could come with us, if you wish. I
don't think it's really your thing though—nobody
under fifty and all we do is play bridge. A dull party
for a lively young thing like yourself. I'm sure if
Patrick doesn't get home you'll find some other way
to console yourself. After all, there are plenty of
young men in town. All old friends of yours, I believe.''

"I'll be just fine, thank you,'' she answered
coldly, pouring herself a cup of coffee with an unsteady hand. ''Why don't you leave as soon as

you're ready? I'd welcome some time alone in my own house.''

"Ungrateful bitch," Ermy murmured malevolently, lifting her overdressed bulk majestically. "I need to get away from this depressing place and all the depressing people in it." She paused and turned to Molly. "And when did you decide to take Patrick into your bed?" she demanded frostily.

Molly stared at her. Ermintrude used to frighten her, she realized. She'd lost her power over her, sometime in the last few days. "When I was sixteen," she replied calmly, turning away.

"You are an ungrateful, scheming little slut," Ermy said boldly. "When I think how I wasted some of the best years of my life guiding you, advising you, trying to teach you a bit about the ways of the world..."

"You did a good job, between you and Lisa," she answered, staring out the kitchen window. The day looked warmer, the winter-dead grass had a faint tinge of color. It was no day for a young man to lie dead. No day for her husband to be in jail. She turned back to her so-called relatives. "It's too late to change the past. When you get back from your visit I think you'd better start making plans to find some other place to live. I think you've worn out your welcome around here a long time ago. You and Willy."

"Listen to me, you conniving little brat!" Aunt Ermy started toward her, grabbing her wrist in a bone-crushing grip. As a matter of pure reflex Molly kicked her in the shins, and Ermy pulled away, shrieking curses. Some of the phrases were rather good, and Molly was sorry she couldn't remember them for later use. Willy hurriedly helped his cousin out of the kitchen, hushing her with words Molly could neither hear nor imagine. By the time they reached the stairs she had quieted down, and the sound of their whispering was barely audible.

"What mischief are they hatching up now?" Mrs. Morse demanded. "If I were you I'd keep an eye on them before they leave. You might find the best silver gone with them if you're not careful."

"Don't worry," Molly said. "I wouldn't trust Aunt Ermy farther than I could throw her, which is about half an inch. And Willy's not any better." She turned to Mrs. Morse. "Why don't you go on home now? Everyone can get their own lunch around here—there's no reason you should wait around for *their* sakes. I'm just going to call the police and then go for a ride. After a few minutes with those two I feel like I need a breath of fresh air."

Mrs. Morse nodded sagely. "I know how you feel. You sure you won't mind being all alone here?"

"Not a bit," Molly lied, smiling bravely. After all, there'd be no one left to hurt her.

SHE WAS OUT for several hours on the back of old Fountain, the mellowest horse in the stable. The police had refused to release any information, either about Toby or Patrick, and Molly had slammed down the phone on the unhelpful Sergeant Stroup in a blazing fury.

Oddly enough, they didn't seem interested in trying to search her blank memory one more time. Maybe they already had the answers, she thought, unnerved. She needed the ride to burn off some of the helpless frustration that swamped her, and she had no intention of spending another minute in the company of her hateful relatives. That last little battle with Aunt Ermy was the final straw.

It was a gorgeous day, giving lie to the storm that raged in her heart. The fresh spring air did its best to convince her that all was right with the world. The budding trees, the daffodils and crocuses, the soft spring smell of wet, warm earth were an intoxicant, and she prayed that when she returned to the old stone house Ermy and Willy would be gone and Patrick would be back.

She should have known the latter would be too much to hope for. The house was very still as she made her way slowly, reluctantly through the barns toward the kitchen door. Her sixth sense, such as it was, was working overtime, and she had the unshakable feeling that something very bad awaited her inside the flagstoned hallways of Winter's Edge.

She opened the door with deceptive boldness. "Anyone home?" she called out, thinking of the day just over a week ago when she first remembered entering this house. It seemed astonishing that so much could have happened in such a short time.

Slowly, bravely, methodically, she went through each room of the house, calling out as she went. By the time she reached the attic she should have been satisfied that the house was empty except for Beastie's slumbering form, and yet she couldn't shake her sense of panic. Of disaster lurking.

She hadn't even had time to think about Toby's death. It felt unreal—that intense light in his eyes suddenly snuffed out. She wanted to mourn, but all she could think about was Patrick.

She went back downstairs, determined to be calmly reasonable as she locked all the doors and windows, whistling tunelessly as she moved through the house. What she was locking them against, she didn't know and refused to try to imagine—she was nervous enough already. The sun was already sinking lower in the sky, and eerie shadows were growing in the spotless corners of the house.

Briskly she walked into the kitchen and made a pot of coffee. Five-thirty. She picked up the discarded newspapers, grabbed a plate of home-baked muffins and went back into the living room to be near her sleeping canine friend.

Someone had already laid a fire, and she lit it, despite the warmth of the late afternoon sun shining through the multi-paned windows. She needed every bit of cheeriness and warmth she could get. Someone had murdered Toby Pentick, and the one person she knew couldn't have done it was the only one in custody. Whoever had killed Toby was most likely the same person who'd been trying to kill her. And here she sat, alone in the house, a perfect sitting duck. The idea was not exactly heartwarming.

Something incriminating was found by Toby's body, Mrs. Morse had said. For some reason her mind went back to the handkerchief still hidden away in the bedside table. The handkerchief with Patrick's initials and the mysterious rust-colored stains. And with a sudden horrid sinking feeling she recognized the short spurt of memory that came rushing back. The handkerchief wasn't an ancient love token. She had found it clasped in her father's murdered hand. And in a last moment of consciousness she had hidden it away from the police's prying eyes. Something incriminating, her brain echoed.

On an impulse she couldn't quite understand she made her way back up to the attic, to the gloom-shrouded shapes of the abandoned furniture. The handkerchief was exactly where she had left it, tucked in the back drawer of the ugly dresser. She stared at the orange, bloodlike streaks thoughtfully, some distant memory teasingly out of reach.

She slowly returned to the living room and the fire, the scrap of incriminating cloth in her hand. Settling back in the chair, she stared straight ahead. Beastie snored beside her, snuffling noisily in his sleep, bringing her back to her senses. If she doubted Patrick, what did she have left? She picked up the newspaper again, determined not to think about it.

The crossword puzzle proved almost too easy, the coffee had none of its usual wakening effects, and the warmth from the fire made her suddenly drowsy. In between clues she fell asleep, the handkerchief clutched in her hand.

Chapter Seventeen

It was an odd sort of dream, even from the beginning. It was too logical, too familiar to be a fantasy. And yet at the beginning it was as pleasant and somehow frightening as most dreams are.

It was her wedding day. She was dressed in the lace and eyelet dress that hung straight down past her shoulders, and the antique veil sat delicately upon her head. Her slanted green-blue eyes were filled with angry tears as Aunt Ermy and Lisa Canning bustled around her, making busy, critical noises.

"You look absolutely lovely, darling," Lisa crooned, arranging the veil about her shoulders. "I'm sure Pat will be most pleasantly surprised."

The bride felt a stab of resentment, one she hid quite well. After all, she had won, hadn't she? He was marrying her, for whatever his reasons. He hadn't waited for Lisa Canning to divorce her gentle-mannered older husband.

"For goodness sake, Molly, smile!" Aunt Ermy ordered in exasperation. "One would think you were going to your funeral instead of to a wedding. It's not as if we all don't know you're in love with him, and have been ever since you were a teenager. I only wonder how you managed to hook him.''

"I was wondering the same thing," Lisa murmured lazily, fingering the opulent hot-house bouquet with the yellow orchids that she and Aunt Ermy had chosen for her. They had wanted to pick the wedding dress too—a dumpy-looking satin creation that had taken their fancy, but on this point she'd had a strange moment of stubbornness. She had taken her little car and spent the day shopping, returning with the simple, old-fashioned dress she now wore, and the slight victory gave her confidence as she watched her pale, nervous face in the mirror of her pink-and-white room.

"You don't think he's in love with you, do you?" Lisa leaned closer. At the betraying expression on the bride's face, Lisa laughed. "Oh, you poor dear, you do! Did he tell you so?"

"No," she whispered, unwilling to confide in the older woman. She had believed, held the idea firmly in her heart of hearts, that underneath his friendly exterior he really cared for her. That he just hadn't realized it yet. Otherwise why would he have asked her to marry him? The money wasn't that important—she would have given it to him anyway, and well he knew it.

"Of course he didn't!" Lisa said in quiet triumph. "That's because, my dear, he loves me. But you know that—heaven knows we've tried to be discreet about our little affair, but word does get around. Just last night he begged me to run off with him, to put a stop to this atrocious masquerade. His very words, my dear—'atrocious masquerade.'" Lisa was lying, but how could the girl have known it was merely the prompting of a feverishly jealous mind? She believed every word.

"He needn't go through with it," Molly muttered sulkily, her unhappiness building. "All he has to do is come and tell me and we'll end it right now."

"With the guests arriving at the church already?" Lisa raised one beautifully molded eyebrow. "Pat doesn't like fusses made, my dear. If you want I could give you quite a few pointers on what Pat does like in a woman. After all, you are going to be his wife. A few little secrets as to what pleases him sexually should help your rather desperate situation, sweetie." Her smile was like a cat's. "No, he won't back down. It was too much wine and passion last night that made him suggest it. He needs your money too much. Winter's Edge means more to him than any woman." Lisa's voice was laced with bitterness, and the bride felt a small stirring of revenge. At least he didn't love her enough either.

Aunt Ermy was strangely silent through all this, watching the scene with satisfaction in her mean little eyes. She was magnificently overdressed as usual, in a powder blue full-length suit with matching turban and eye shadow. Attached to her noble breast was a cluster of gardenias—the scent overpowered the lighter fragrances in Molly's bouquet and made her slightly ill.

"Before your wedding night, my dear, I feel I

ought to warn you," Lisa continued, her ripe, full mouth a crimson curve against her artificially tanned skin. "He has certain sexual...shall we say, aberrations...that might frighten a young girl if she isn't warned—"

"Enough!" Molly cried suddenly, angrily. "I'm leaving now." She grabbed her bouquet and headed for the door. "I'm getting married in less than an hour," she told them coolly, taking pleasure in reminding Lisa. "It wouldn't do for the bride to be late."

"But the limousine hasn't arrived yet," Aunt Ermy protested.

"I'm driving myself," she answered them with icy calm, recognizing the hatred behind their tender concern. Wondering why she had never seen that hatred before. "*You* can ride in the limousine."

"And what will Pat think of this little outburst?" Lisa asked slyly. "You know how he hates things to be changed at the last minute."

"Pat," she said slowly, "can go to hell."

THE WIND BLEW her hair wildly as she sped toward the church, driving twenty and thirty miles above the speed limit. She had taken off the veil and stuffed it behind the seat with her bouquet. She very carefully didn't cry—it had taken her over half an hour to apply her makeup and she didn't propose to ruin it on *his* account. "Bastard," she said out loud, savoring the sound of the word. "Bastard, bastard, bastard!" she shouted to the blue, blue skies.

So he had spent the eve of their wedding with

another woman, had he? And what right had she to complain? He had made her no promises, not even a word of affection when he had made his startling proposal. And she had jumped at it, because for seven long years he had been the only thing in her life that had mattered. Even if things had been strained between them since Jared had died and the terms of the will made public, she'd hoped, she'd prayed, that at least his tolerant affection for her remained. And that her love for him would be enough to support her.

"Not anymore," she said grimly, speeding over the rutted macadam roads. "Not anymore."

Her wedding passed in a daze. Lisa Canning stood beside her, her gleaming eyes carefully lowered, only the small smile that hovered around her full lips hinting at the pleasure she found in the uncomfortable situation.

Aunt Ermy cried, and kissed her cold face. "Molly, dear, you make such a lovely bride. Who would have thought you'd have the dignity to carry it off? Try to smile, dear." A sharp pinch accompanied the admonition, and she could barely restrain a little outcry. Aunt Ermy was fond of delivering painful little pinches for improper behavior.

And so she was very gay. The reception was one lavish feast, with the bride dancing and flirting and smiling and laughing and kissing everyone there. Except her husband. With her husband she was even shriller, even gayer, desperate to hide the mortal blow Lisa had given her. His dark blue eyes followed her, doubt turning into a slow rage that built as the hours went on, until, when it was time to leave, he snapped at his child bride.

She shouted something obscene and very nasty back to him and fled the hall. Then she drove away, back to Winter's Edge in her bright red sports car, leaving her husband fuming with rage. A perfect setup for Lisa Canning.

That night seemed endless. She sat in her huge, soft bed with the pink satin sheets and waited for him, dressed so carefully in her bridal nightgown of sheer gauze. It made her itch. And she rehearsed the things she'd say to him. How she'd apologize for making a fool of him in front of all those people. How they would lie there and talk about their marriage, and come to some sort of understanding of what they meant to each other. Things they should have talked about before the wedding, but she had been frightened of scaring him off.

The hours passed, and he didn't come. Then she planned the things she'd say to him, demanding where he'd been, why he'd left her for so long. And then they would forgive each other and make love in this soft, too elegant bed that Lisa had picked for them, and everything would be fine.

And when morning finally came, and Patrick hadn't bothered to come to his foolishly virginal bride, a core of anger grew and hardened in her, fed with the hurt of his rejection and the humiliation of having been left on her wedding night. She had saved herself for him, because no other man would ever do for her; she had waited for Patrick to want her. But he hadn't wanted her.

From that night on she locked her door against him. A locked door he had barely seemed to notice, much less mind. The warmth and friendliness that had existed between them before their marriage was gone and in its place was a hurtful, implacable hatred. That was very close to love.

Until the night when it had all become too much for her. She was a stranger in her own house—it seemed that Patrick found her presence an annoyance, and the others considered her a selfish little slut. All except one of them, who was her friend.

The dream then became fraught with danger, and Molly stirred in the armchair, trying to wake up. She didn't like this. She didn't want to remember, to relive what happened next. But the dream moved on.

That friend had been the only one she could confide in. But he was shadowy and unclear; even his voice seemed to come from far away, telling her to leave Patrick, to run away where no one could ever find her. If she went with her father, taking her money, he would see to it that Patrick would never use her again.

She tried to see him clearly through the mists, but he remained maddeningly out of reach...until that night when old Fred Canning finally succumbed to his cancer, and her friend told her that Patrick was going to divorce her.

She went out with him to the far barn, where Patrick kept his breeding stock, and watched with numb, drugged horror as he set fire to the place after striking poor old Ben and leaving him in a pool of blood.

"What are you doing?" she screamed at him. "You said you were going to help me leave here!"

"You are leaving here, Molly dear. You're leaving here for good, in that fire." He started dragging her screaming, kicking body toward that inferno, the heat scorching their faces, and whatever he had put in her drink earlier made her unable to stop him.

And then, before he could shove her struggling, helpless body down into the funeral pyre, they heard shouts from nearby, and the slow scream of the fire engine. He cursed, and loosened his hold for a moment, and she pulled away and ran, blindly, hysterically, through the woods that no one knew as well as she did, back to the deserted house. She grabbed a handful of clothes, took all the spare money Patrick kept in the petty cash box, climbed into her car, and drove all night long, her terror fighting the effects of the sleeping pill he'd given her. When she reached New York state she checked into a rundown motel and slept for eighteen hours.

HE WAS THERE in the room. If she opened her eyes the shadows would pass away and she would see the man who wanted to kill her quite clearly. But then, she thought craftily, if she kept her eyes closed he might disappear and she would be safe. All in all, it was a problem, but with her newfound courage she slowly opened her downcast blue-green eyes and stared at the crumpled handkerchief in her hand.

With its streaks of orange hair dye. She raised her
eyes.

"Hello, Uncle Willy."

Chapter Eighteen

"You don't seem very surprised to see me," he said, and Molly stirred in the chair, determined not to show for a minute the absolute terror he instilled in her. She remembered everything now, and she desperately wished she didn't.

"Oh, Molly." He moved forward into the room, and once again she was aware of the lingering cruelty in his soft pink face, the cruelty she'd refused to recognize in the past week of blessed forgetfulness. "I've told you before you never were much of an actress. You've remembered."

"Yes." Her voice came out in a rusty croak, and she cleared it hastily.

Beastie snored loudly beside her, and she tugged silently at his collar. "It won't do you any good, my dear," Willy said smoothly, running a slightly trembling hand over his carroty strands of hair. "He's drugged. I decided I didn't want him interfering with my plans tonight—he's too fond of you, you know."

"And what exactly are your plans for tonight?"

She sounded almost unnaturally calm. She'd been through too much in the last few days, the last few weeks. All she could do was pull this false serenity around her, watching him while she thought feverishly of escape.

"Now, now, Molly, I'm sure you can imagine." He seated himself in the chair opposite her and crossed his legs, at home and urbane. "I'm going to have to kill you." He sighed. "I suppose I should tell you that it grieves me, but quite frankly, it doesn't bother me in the slightest. You've been an annoying little pain in the rear ever since Jared brought you home, and your indestructibility is absolutely infuriating."

"Why do you want to kill me?"

"For the oldest reason in the world, my dear. Money. You have lots of it, I want it. It's really quite simple." For once the man was quite sober, and the effect had a horrifying charm to it.

"My money goes to Patrick if I die." She couldn't keep a note of desperation from her voice. She was strong, but Uncle Willy, despite his alcohol-induced flabbiness, had overpowered her before, the night of the barn fire, and he could doubtless do it again.

"It does, my dear. But not if he's convicted of murder. And it looks pleasantly as if it will work out that way. I had planned to make it a triple play, as they say in baseball. You, your father and Toby. But I might have to settle on a suicide for you."

"You killed my father," she stated flatly.

He nodded benevolently. "Well, no. Actually I

arranged for Toby to do it, but I was there, watching. I've learned it never pays to leave important tasks to underlings. People need supervision nowadays— they have no incentive. Toby was eager enough to please, but he wasn't very good at improvising. I see you're clutching my important piece of evidence. I was very distressed that Patrick's handkerchief wasn't found with the body, Molly. That upset a great many careful plans."

"It had your hair dye on it." She held up the square of linen.

She was pleased to see his ruddy complexion turn a sickly pale. "Good heavens, how careless of me! And how very fortunate that you thought to save your husband. Fate has been on my side after all, it seems. Things should work out very well this way, very well indeed."

"We were bringing you that money." Memories were flooding back at a terrifying, dizzying rate. "Why did you have to kill him?"

"It was necessary. Your father, petty little swindler that he was, knew what was going on the minute you turned up. He thought he could blackmail me for half of that money. You didn't know that, did you? He soon found out otherwise. That was my only mistake, Molly dear." He eyed his hands reflectively. "I thought that blow on your head killed you. Crushed your stubborn little skull. I should have known you were far too hardheaded. Imagine my displeasure when the police called and you were still alive. And no handkerchief! I thought all my plans had failed dismally." He shook his head sadly.

"But you had that convenient loss of memory that no one believed, and now, everything has worked out splendidly. Just splendidly." He sighed.

"Just splendidly," she echoed in a daze.

"Ah, I can see you had some of your ginger ale tonight. It's much harder to hide drugs in soft drinks, you realize. Tonight it's just a strong sedative. You're too willful, my dear. But it's already slowed you down, I'm pleased to notice."

She hadn't touched the ginger ale. She looked up at Uncle Willy with feigned blankness.

"I don't plan to make it painful," he added. "As much as you've annoyed me, I'm basically a decent human being. I try not to hold grudges. And I can be fairly certain that no one has the faintest idea that I had a hand in either your father's death or Toby's. For one thing I have no motive—or not as strong a one as your dear husband. And for another, my dear Ermy will provide me with excellent alibis. Did you know, for example, that right now I am visiting our old friends the Sturbridges over in Devon? They had to go out on a previous engagement, but when they left I was there and when they return I will still be there. And there will be one less member of the exalted Winters family in the meantime."

There was a sneer in his voice as he rose and poured himself a stiff drink. His hands were suddenly still, unlike the usual mild tremor that afflicted him. Just another part of his elaborate charade.

"And what if they don't convict Patrick?" she asked, speaking in a deliberately thickened voice.

He shrugged his shoulders. "That's no problem,

really. He won't marry again. He's in love with you, my dear. We all knew it, even if you were too heartsick and adolescent to realize it. Your untimely death by suicide will deal him a mortal blow. He'll continue to support Ermy and me because he's foolishly generous, and in a few years he'll meet with a recalcitrant horse or faulty brakes. He does drive too fast, you know. Such an angry, impetuous man. You could have been the making of him, but alas, that isn't to be. We can wait, once our goal is in sight. Infinite patience, that's what's required in a really first-class criminal mind." He drank deeply from his drink and stared into the fire. "Yes, my dear Molly, I consider myself a criminal, and I am proud of it. An ordinary man couldn't do what I've done. I can plan extraordinarily complicated schemes, I can kill when it's necessary, without compunction, and that all requires a truly high degree of dedication and skill."

"I don't understand what Toby had to do with this," she said, trying to keep Willy talking while she searched for any possible avenue of escape. The keys were in the car—she could probably run faster than he could, especially if she took him by surprise. He thought she was falling into a drugged stupor; instead the adrenaline was surging through her body. "Why would he be willing to kill? And why would you turn around and kill him?"

"Toby?" he said blankly. "Toby was becoming somewhat of a problem. He was the one who tried to kill you by the ruins, you know. And he was all set to crush your clever little brain in when he

tripped up the horse. If Patrick hadn't made his untimely appearance it would all be over with, and you
would have been spared a lot of needless fuss. But
then, that's what life's all about, isn't it? Needless
fuss.''

He swirled his rapidly disappearing drink with
one fat, pale finger. ''That's a good lesson to learn,
my dear. Never take a psycho into partnership with
you. Toby was not what you'd call well-balanced.
He'd always been consumed with a strange passion
for you, and when you married Patrick it tipped him
over the edge. He decided since he couldn't have
you then nobody could. I'm afraid finding out your
sexual liaison with your husband rather set the seal
on his...problems. When he failed to strangle you
last night he was going to come back with a gun,
and that seemed far too sloppy. I suppose I could
have taken the chance and let him do it. I could have
hoped he wouldn't talk and just let all my work be
handled by a poor deranged boy. But chances are
not my style at all. Not at all. So I took care of him
myself.'' He sighed heavily. ''If you hadn't gone
creeping off to Patrick's bed I could have finished
what Toby had so sloppily started. The coroner
probably wouldn't have noticed that Toby's death
preceded yours.''

''And you left something incriminating of Patrick's by his side? As you tried to do with my father?'' she questioned, watching him as he rose and
made his way to the bar.

''Naturally. I had had the foresight to arm myself
ahead of time with another of his handkerchiefs and

his watch. There's no way he'll be released—the police are an awfully gullible lot. That ox Stroup would just love to lock Pat up and have you all alone out here. But when he comes to call he'll find Pat's poor wife dead by her own hand, and he'll…''

She was on her feet and out of the room before he could turn around. She slammed open the front door and ran out into the cool night air. A light rain was falling, and the sounds of Uncle Willy's furious pursuit were unmistakable. She raced toward the garage, dodging through doorways, as she heard him come closer and closer, his heaving, panting breath loud in the stillness.

Finally she reached the old van. The night was oddly silent—Uncle Willy must have gone in the wrong direction. She jumped in the car and reached for the ignition.

The keys were gone. She felt around on the floor, in the glove compartment, fright and desperation making her oblivious to the threat moving up behind her. When she straightened up she looked directly into Willy's pale, murderous eyes.

Like a fool she sat there, too numb with horror to lock the doors against him. He yanked her out of the driver's seat, insane fury mixing with some ghastly trace of amusement.

''I warned you I consider myself a master criminal,'' he said in his soft voice, his pale fat hands on her arm, squeezing with surprising strength. ''You just made a fool of me, Molly. Even though I had the foresight to remove the keys, you shouldn't have gotten this far. You didn't drink anything at all tonight, did you? You thought you could fool me. Most annoying of you. And it would have been a waste of time—the van isn't working properly, remember? No," he said, dragging her back through the barns and the courtyard, into the kitchen, "I'm afraid you're going to have to be punished for this. The loss of my dignity will come very dear. I was going to try to make it easy for you, for old times' sake, but now it's going to hurt. It's going to hurt quite a bit." His eyes glistened and Molly noticed he was drooling slightly.

For a moment she thought she saw a flash of light in the distance, but it was gone before she could look further, and she didn't want to alert her would-be murderer. Help was highly unlikely. If she was to stay alive it was up to her, and right now her chances didn't look too promising.

"How are you going to do it?" she asked him humbly when they reached the living room once more and he'd shoved her down into the chair.

He chuckled pleasantly, running his pale, sluglike hand across his mussed orange strands. "You'll be found hanging from one of the rafters in the attic. And it should take quite a while to find you—a type-written note will serve to distract everyone for a few days. Until you begin to smell, my dear." He sat and reached for his drink. "I had meant to be generous and snap your little neck with a quick jerk of my wrists so that you'd only have a moment of blinding pain before it was all over." He smiled through the cheerful firelight, and Beastie snored blissfully on. "But now, my dear, I'm going to strangle you, slowly, so I can watch your eyes bulge out, watch you gasp and scream for mercy, watch you pleading as I rip your life away with my bare hands.'' It all sounded like a recipe: detailed, but simple and effective.

Shuddering uncontrollably, she let her hand trail nervelessly, and noticed, an aching fraction of an inch out of her reach, the lovely old brass-handled fire tools. He would notice in a second if she appeared to reach for them, and her one final chance of salvation would be gone.

Willy looked at his watch in a businesslike fashion. ''I'm afraid it's getting late, my dear,'' he announced affably. ''This is pleasant but I do have to allow enough time to get back before my hosts return.'' He rose, and came toward her slowly, very slowly. She watched him out of hooded eyes, concentrating desperately on the fire poker just out of reach, thinking of Patrick, and of poor, sick, dead Toby. Of her father, whom she'd barely known. She'd thought she could go to him for help, for a place to hide from Willy and the danger, a place to hide from the husband who hated her. Instead he'd been ready to betray her for money. But in the end he was the one who was betrayed.

Willy moved closer, running a quick tongue over his dry, flabby lips, his eyes moist and shining, his fat pale fingers twitching.

And then a sound, the briefest of unexpected noises broke in the room. He whirled around, his back presented for only a second. It was all Molly needed. Without an instant's hesitation she smashed him over the head with the lovely brass-handled fire poker, the fastidious orange hairs providing no padding. His squat body sank to the floor in a curious attitude of surprise. She looked up and met the astonished deep blue eyes of her husband, followed closely by Lieutenant Ryker and his posse.

After a moment Patrick broke the stillness. "How the hell," he asked in a faintly disgruntled tone of voice, "am I supposed to save you when you prove entirely capable of rescuing yourself?"

She shrugged, and smiled, took one step toward him and quite calmly passed out on the body of dear Uncle Willy.

Epilogue

She slept in his arms that night, curled up snugly against his body as if that was where she belonged. Patrick lay beside her, drifting in and out of sleep, his arms tight and possessive around her.

He'd tried to reason with her. "I'm too old for you," he'd said. "I have too foul a temper."

"I'm mature for my age," she'd said, an arrant lie, as she bit his shoulder. "And I'm fairly grumpy myself."

"I should never have married you," he tried to tell her, later, when she was licking his navel. "I took advantage of you. I knew you had a crush on me, that you'd do anything for me..."

"I would," she agreed, moving her head lower.

His voice grew tight and husky. "But it's not fair to you."

"Let me decide what's fair," she said.

"You'll find someone better suited to you."

"There isn't anyone better for me."

"You'll regret it."

Her mouth was too busy to reply to such a pat-

ently ridiculous statement, and he found he couldn't
manage to come up with any more arguments for
the time being. But later, when they were curled
tight around each other, he slid his hands through
her thick tangle of wheat-colored hair and tilted her
face up to his. She looked sleepy, sated, immensely
pleased with herself, and he didn't want to care that
much.

"I won't hold you here," he said in a harsh, quiet
voice.

She stared at him, her eyes wide. "You can't
make me leave you." She reached up her own hands
to cup his cheeks, and her voice was intense. "Don't
you love me, Patrick?"

He'd never meant to tell her. He's always thought
it would take unfair advantage of her. But there was
no way he could not answer her simple, heartfelt
question.

"Completely," he said.

She smiled, a bright, tear-filled smile. "I know,"
she said.

And he wondered if he'd just made the worst mistake of his entire life.

WHEN MOLLY WOKE UP the next morning he was
gone. She hadn't felt him leave. She could hear Mrs.
Morse humming to herself in the kitchen below—
Patrick had left the door ajar. Mrs. Morse was in a
very good mood. She was singing out of tune and
quite loudly.

Molly jumped out of Patrick's bed and stretched
luxuriously. Bright sunlight was pouring in the open

windows, and it seemed as if winter was finally coming to a close. It was good to be alive on this April morning, though she doubted poor Willy felt so. She had only managed to daze him, and he was now unhappily incarcerated in the county jail, awaiting arraignment.

She showered and dressed quickly in cutoff jeans and the tightest T-shirt she owned. She wanted to see Patrick. To see whether the slowly burgeoning trust and friendliness survived outside the bedroom walls. To see whether he still knew that he loved her.

And yet she was almost afraid to find out. If he turned that cold, stony face on her once more she didn't think she could bear it.

"And how are you this fine morning?" Mrs. Morse greeted her with almost tasteless good cheer, considering the circumstances. Bringing coffee and muffins to the table, she pulled out a chair invitingly. "Eat, for goodness sake!" she ordered. "Patrick told me all about your fright last night—you need rest and good food after an ordeal like that!" She shook her head meaningfully. "Willy confessed all nice and neat when he saw it was useless. No, we won't have him to worry us ever again. They'll lock him away for hundreds of years, you mark my words. I'm only thinking it's a shame they don't use capital punishment more often." She paused for breath. "And as for your Aunt Ermy, why she just disappeared off the face of the earth, as far as anyone can tell. Doesn't seem like they'll ever find her, more's the pity. What's the matter, child, don't you have any appetite?''

Molly shook her head and smiled nervously. "I don't care whether they find Ermy or not," she said truthfully. "As long as she keeps away from here it doesn't matter to me what she does with herself. I don't imagine she was anything more than a pawn in Uncle Willy's game.''

Mrs. Morse sniffed. "That's as may be. She was still one of the meanest women I've ever known, and don't you doubt it. Still, I suppose you're right—as long as she's gone that's all that matters. It still horrifies me to think of the years that have gone by with them living here as friendly as you please, all the time planning such wickedness.'' She shook her graying head with wonder. "Come on now, dearie, eat something. You need to get some meat on those bones.'' Her eyes reflected a mild disapproval for the scantiness of Molly's clothing.

"Where's Patrick?'' she asked suddenly, the suspense unbearable. Before any more time passed she had to find out what his attitude toward her might be.

"He was out in the yard last time I looked. He said to tell you that you and he would have to go into town later on to give statements to the police...'' Her voice trailed off as Molly ran out the door.

The sun was pouring down, the first really hot day of the year, and she had to squint her eyes against the glare. There was the faintest hint of a breeze, and it blew her hair in her face. She pushed it away impatiently, looking for him, half afraid of what she'd see when she looked into his eyes.

She saw him first, his lean, strong body bent over some piece of riding tack, his eyes narrowed in concentration, his black hair curling around his neck in an endearing way that made her long to reach out and touch it. So far she hadn't quite dared.

She moved closer, casting a shadow across his work, and he looked up swiftly. ''Hullo,'' she said rather breathlessly, trying to hide her nervousness, all the while listening to the pounding of her heart, the jumping of her nerves, her flat out panic that this was all going to end in disaster.

He stood up, looking at her for a moment, his face cool and expressionless. And then his eyes warmed. He reached for her, and without thinking she ran into his arms.

His mouth came down on hers with such casual, automatic intimacy that she knew it was going to be all right. She reached out and ran her fingers through the tangle of hair at the back of his neck. He drew back slightly, and his smile was brighter than the blazing sun.

''Hullo, yourself,'' he said. ''I love you.''

And winter was over at last.

HARLEQUIN®
SUPERROMANCE®

By the Year 2000: BABY!

What have *you* resolved to do by the year 2000?
These three women are having babies!

Susan Kennedy's plan is to have a baby by the time she's forty—in the year 2000. But the only man she can imagine as the father of her child is her ex-husband, Michael!
MY BABIES AND ME by Tara Taylor Quinn
Available in October 1999

Nora Holloway is determined to adopt the baby who suddenly appears in her life! And then the baby's uncle shows up....
DREAM BABY by Ann Evans
Available in November 1999

By the year 2000, the Irving Trust will end, unless Miranda has a baby. She doesn't think there's much likelihood of that—until she meets Joseph Wallace.
THE BABY TRUST by Bobby Hutchinson
Available in December 1999

Available at your favorite retail outlet.

HARLEQUIN®
Makes any time special ™

Visit us at www.romance.net

HSR2000B

Harlequin is proud to introduce:

...Where Every Man Has His Price!

Lost Springs Ranch was famous for turning young mavericks into good men. Word that the ranch was in financial trouble sent a herd of loyal bachelors stampeding back to Wyoming to put themselves on the auction block.

This is a brand-new 12-book continuity, which includes some of Harlequin's most talented authors.

Don't miss the first book,
Husband for Hire by Susan Wiggs.
It will be at your favorite retail outlet in July 1999.

HARLEQUIN®
Makes any time special ™